"Tell me you don't want me... that you
aren't attracted to me any more," Micah demanded.

She couldn't, so she didn't. She glared at him
instead, forgetting he couldn't see her, then murmured, "You have the power to hurt me, Micah. I
wouldn't survive an affair with you."

He groaned, then brought her against his muscled chest, molded her against him so that she could
feel his heartbeat against her body. "I wouldn't hurt
you for anything in the world. Don't you know that
yet?"

Dazed by the currents of sensation spiraling
through her body, Bliss wondered if she knew anything at all. She'd never felt more vulnerable or
shaken by her desire for a man. She twisted in his
arms, but when he claimed her lips, his assault on
her senses was the most tender thing she'd ever
experienced. No man had ever wanted her with such
intense desire. Her body throbbed with the need to
abandon her battle against the attraction she felt for
Micah. Even as she cursed his power over her, she
craved him as a lover.

"Tell me, Bliss," he urged in a low voice so
filled with erotic tension that she wanted to burrow
beneath his skin and stay there forever. "Tell me
how I'm supposed to walk away from you. . . ."

WHAT ARE *LOVESWEPT* ROMANCES?

They are stories of true romance and touching emotion. We believe those two very important ingredients are constants in our highly sensual and very believable stories in the LOVESWEPT line. Our goal is to give you, the reader, stories of consistently high quality that may sometimes make you laugh, sometimes make you cry, but are always fresh and creative and contain many delightful surprises within their pages.

Most romance fans read an enormous number of books. Those they truly love, they keep. Others may be traded with friends and soon forgotten. We hope that each LOVESWEPT romance will be a treasure—a "keeper." We will always try to publish

LOVE STORIES YOU'LL NEVER FORGET
BY AUTHORS YOU'LL ALWAYS REMEMBER

The Editors

Loveswept 634

HEARTBREAKER

LAURA
TAYLOR

BANTAM BOOKS

NEW YORK · TORONTO · LONDON · SYDNEY · AUCKLAND

HEARTBREAKER

A Bantam Book / August 1993

If you would be interested in receiving protective vinyl covers for your
Loveswept books, please write to this address for information:

Loveswept
Bantam Books
P.O. Box 985
Hicksville, NY 11802

ISBN 0-553-44346-1

Published simultaneously in the United States and Canada

Bantam Books are published by Bantam Books, a division of Bantam Doubleday Dell Publishing Group, Inc. Its trademark, consisting of the words
"Bantam Books" and the portrayal of a rooster, is Registered in U.S. Patent
and Trademark Office and in other countries. Marca Registrada. Bantam
Books, 1540 Broadway, New York, New York 10036.

PRINTED IN THE UNITED STATES OF AMERICA

OPM   0 9 8 7 6 5 4 3 2 1

For Celeste De Blasis, my favorite icon.
Happy 20th Anniversary

HEARTBREAKER

ONE

Bliss Rowland spotted an imperfection in the clay that she couldn't ignore. She dipped her fingers into a bowl of water and then lightly smoothed one fingertip across the base of a large sculpture mounted on a pedestal in the center of her studio. She smiled as she stepped back and surveyed the subtle change.

A life-size impressionistic piece, the sculpture had flowing curves and hollows that represented the reclining figure of a naked woman. Although partially submerged by an advancing tide, the woman was at peace with the ebb and flow of the nearby sea.

Bliss knew she was her own worst critic. She demanded the very best of herself, and she never settled for less. She also understood and accepted her compulsive devotion to her sculpting as a consequence of her tumultuous childhood and adolescence. She had created order out of chaos, primarily within the confines of her mind. Her ability to focus, as well as her extraordinary talent, showed now in the results of a grueling year of work.

Bliss felt physically depleted as her gaze swept the spacious studio that housed a dozen original sculptures. She cared little about the fatigue that caused faint shadows beneath her green eyes, the disheveled state of her short, curly black hair, or the loose fit of her clothes. She apologized to no one for sleeping only when she was too exhausted to do anything else or if she missed regular meals when she prepared for a one-woman show.

She circled the pedestal one last time. Drying her fingers on the hem of her T-shirt, Bliss slowly completed her inspection. She paused finally, lifted her arms to stretch the kinks from her shoulders and neck, and then exhaled softly. The satisfied sound that escaped her blended with the fragrant Saint Thomas breeze that sighed through the palm trees in the courtyard that separated her studio from the main house on the private estate that she called home.

Whatever the critics decided about this collection, Bliss knew that she'd retain her pride in her achievement. She felt a deep sense of satisfaction about each sculpture on its own merits, though she was also pleased that the international art community had long ago acknowledged her as a sculptor of originality, a risk-taker who challenged the observer to explore both the subtleties and the boldness of her creations.

The phone rang, jarring her from her concentration. She stiffened the instant she heard the voice on the other end of the line.

"This is your father, Bliss."

Caution saturated her as she said, "Hello, Dad. How are you?"

"I'm fine," Cyrus Rowland answered.

Bliss heard the tension in the presidential envoy's cultured voice. "Is something wrong, Dad?"

"Why do you ask?"

"You rarely call," she reminded him with the candor that had evolved between them over the years.

"Is that a criticism, Bliss?"

"Hardly. Just an observation."

"Do you remember Micah Holbrook?"

Startled, Bliss said, "Of course. How could I not remember him?" She silently acknowledged that she'd measured every man she'd ever met against Micah Holbrook, and no one had ever made the grade. No one.

"He's in the hospital in D.C."

Bliss closed her eyes. An ache lodged in her heart and throbbed like a dull wound. "Will he be all right?"

"That's open for debate."

"What happened?"

"I can't go into the details, Bliss."

"Some things never change, do they?" she remarked. *What do you want from me, Dad?* "He probably doesn't remember me, but I hope you'll give him my best wishes for a speedy recovery."

"I'm sending Micah to the estate."

She gripped the phone. "Why?"

"He needs the environment for his convalescence."

"Dad, I'm less than a month from my next show."

"I realize that. Knowing you, though, the work is already done."

How, Bliss wondered, did an absentee father know the details of her life? "I just finished the final piece for the collection this morning," she admitted.

"He helped you when you needed him. I want you to help him now."

"That was a long time ago. I was seventeen years old, for heaven's sake."

"He saved your life. At the very least, you owe him the hospitality of the estate. Besides, you know better than most what he's going through right now."

Bliss remembered more clearly than she wanted to the blast that had nearly destroyed an entire London street and had taken countless lives on a warm summer morning. Trapped in the rubble of a fashionable dress shop, she had struggled to free herself. A twenty-seven-year-old American naval officer had rescued her, shielding her from the carnage of an IRA terrorist bombing as he'd carried her to a waiting ambulance.

"Did you hear me?"

"I know he saved my life."

"And now he needs your help," Cyrus pressed.

"Why does he need *my* help? Surely there are better places for him than Saint Thomas. His doctors must want to keep him . . ."

Her father cut in, "I'm worried about him, Bliss. They can treat his body, but not his spirit. The surgery to restore his vision was highly experimental. He knows the failure rate is close to seventy percent, and he's angry and frightened."

"Like Mom," she whispered. Her mother's diabetes had robbed her of her vision.

"Yes."

"What about his family? Wouldn't he prefer to be around people he knows and trusts?"

"He refuses to allow anyone to contact them. His father's health isn't the best."

"How did it happen?" she asked again, firming her tone to let him know that this time she expected an answer.

"The car bomb in Central America last month."

"Was he one of the men who pulled you to safety?" She recalled the accounts she'd read in the newspaper about the explosion that had almost killed her father.

"Yes."

"Why didn't you call me after it happened?" she asked quietly. "Didn't you think I'd want to know if you were all right?"

"You sound like your mother now."

Bliss consciously kept her voice even. "Mother is dead. She has been for a long time. I have a life. I'm tired, Dad. This show's important to me. I've spent the last year preparing for it. I don't know how much good I'd be to anyone else right now."

He cleared his throat. "Bliss, please do this for me. We both owe him a great deal."

The "please" got her. She couldn't recall the last time her father had said the word to her. Like most men accustomed to wielding power on a global basis, he ordered and demanded. He spoke for presidents. He confronted dictators and brought them to heel. He negotiated treaties and ended wars. And he'd always made his daughter feel like an intruder in his life, until she learned not to seek his approval or attention. In short, Cyrus Rowland was a law unto himself.

"His well-being is that important to you?"

"Yes. You're strong enough to handle him right now. I trust your instincts and your judgment where he's concerned."

His praise shocked her. "All right, Dad."

"Thank you. All the appropriate arrangements have been made. Members of my personal household staff and a security contingent will arrive with him. Everyone's familiar with the layout of the estate except Micah."

"Is he vulnerable?" she asked in response to the mention of security personnel.

Accustomed to the need to guarantee the safety of government officials like her father, Bliss still didn't like the idea of people lurking about her home with weapons at the ready. She tolerated the presence of armed security during her father's infrequent visits to the family estate, or when she acted as his hostess as he entertained a foreign dignitary. Cyrus hadn't come to the estate in almost two years, and the last diplomat she'd entertained for him had turned out to be a playboy she wished she'd never met.

"A threat is possible," Cyrus finally said.

"Micah has spent most of his career with Naval Intelligence. He's worked several highly classified missions, and a man makes enemies in those situations. Enough said?"

"More than enough." Bliss hesitated for a moment, then continued, "He's a friend, isn't he, not just someone who works for you?"

Cyrus laughed. "Try not to hold it against him, Bliss."

She didn't laugh, feeling sad that her father seemed more at ease with friendships that evolved through his work than his family relationships.

"When will he arrive?"

"This afternoon."

Bliss said good-bye and recradled the telephone, shaking her head in disbelief. This afternoon? She wanted to groan. Instead, she returned her attention to the sculpture on the pedestal in the center of her studio. She drew from the symmetry of her creation the strength and inner calm she knew she would need as she faced Micah Holbrook for the first time in eleven years.

Several hours later, Bliss stepped out onto the covered patio as she heard the sound of a helicopter. She watched the aircraft touch down on the back lawn of the estate. An expanse of perfectly manicured grass, it separated the mansion from the turquoise waters of the Caribbean.

Uniformed men spilled out of the interior of the helicopter. She recognized several members of her father's household staff, and she assumed the armed men composed the security contingent.

Micah was the last person to exit the helicopter. He reminded her of a brawny Viking adventurer, and she was pleased that the years had treated him kindly. If anything, Bliss decided as she studied him, he seemed more ruggedly masculine than ever.

She registered the rigid set of his shoulders. His military bearing also showed in his posture, despite his casual attire of slacks, a polo shirt, and leather deck shoes. Bliss remained motionless as two uniformed men stationed themselves on either side of him. Well over six feet in height, broad-shouldered, and narrow hipped, Micah dwarfed his companions.

She sensed the depth of his resentment when he reluctantly placed his hand on the shoulder of one of the men. His long-legged stride appeared confident, but even as she silently blessed the landscaper who'd designed the level, open stretch of lawn, she recalled her mother's fear of embarrassing herself in front of strangers if she stumbled or fell.

Bliss hated seeing Micah forced to depend on others, but she knew he had to come to terms with the reality that he might never regain his sight. Squaring her slender shoulders, she tried to ignore her accelerating heartbeat and racing pulse as Micah approached her. Memories of the crush she'd had on him while still a teenager stirred in her heart and mind, but she chased them away.

Bliss felt an unexpected desire to sculpt Micah's likeness, to capture the definitive lines of his strong-featured face in clay. She'd tried several times over the years, but she'd given up in frustration, not trusting her memory to do him justice. Although she understood why he wore sunglasses, she wished he hadn't felt the need to cover his bandaged eyes.

She wanted to see as much of his face as possible. Her fingertips tingled with the need to trace the contours of his strong brow, high cheekbones, hard cheeks, and the aggressive chin that made him look willful and stubborn. She remembered that he was both. Bliss closed her hands into fists, fearful she might indulge the impulses she felt as he drew nearer.

Her breath caught as a sudden storm of emotions swept over her. The desire to protect herself came out of nowhere and collided with the rashness of her desire. She calmed herself with effort, assuming the role of gracious hostess with a smile that felt stiff and unnatural.

She felt shaken by her unanticipated need to draw Micah into her arms and hold him but within seconds managed to regain her composure. Bliss had a strength of will that invariably surprised people who assumed her petite body and delicate facial features were signs of a fragile character. She couldn't help wondering now if Micah Holbrook would make that same mistake.

Stepping aside, Bliss silently invited her guests into the foyer of the main house with an elegant sweep of her hand. She followed them, pausing in the center of the high-ceilinged room dominated by a gleaming crystal chandelier and a marble staircase that led to the upper level of the mansion.

"Welcome to Saint Thomas, gentlemen. For those of you who don't know me, my name is Bliss Rowland."

She immediately sensed the fury emanating from Micah. It seemed to roll off him in invisible waves, encompassing everything and everyone in its path. Bliss deliberately ignored his hostility. "Some of you have been here before, so please settle in and reacquaint yourselves with the mansion. The two upstairs wings should accommodate all of you, but I'll leave it to you to sort out the sleeping arrangements.

Aside from the studio on the opposite side of the courtyard, you have the run of the estate."

She approached Micah as she spoke. She knew she startled him when she took his hand. He flinched, but Bliss ignored his reaction and laced their fingers together as though they were old friends. "I'll escort Captain Holbrook to his suite."

"Ma'am I'm supposed to . . ."

She smiled at the young man wearing a corpsman's insignia who stood beside Micah. "Please?"

Instantly charmed, he flushed. "Yes, ma'am."

"May I depend on you to take care of his luggage?"

"Of course, ma'am."

"Thank you all." Bliss waited for the others to disperse before speaking to Micah. Once they stood alone in the sprawling foyer, she asked, "How was your trip?"

"Long."

He doesn't remember me, she realized, a combination of relief and disappointment mingling within her. She took a moment to remind herself that most men wouldn't remember a mousy seventeen-year-old girl for eleven years, then recalled Cyrus's admission that Micah had been involved in numerous covert missions for Naval Intelligence, and concluded that more recent violent events had eclipsed for him the terrorist assault on the London shopping district.

"I'm not a nurse," she said, "but I am your hostess during your stay at Rowland House. Cyrus called earlier today. He explained your situation."

Micah said nothing.

Bliss smoothed her fingertips over their joined hands. She felt the clench of his strong fingers. "I'll familiarize you with the mansion and the grounds of the estate. You'll need to try to relax and trust me, which is a lot to ask of you right now, I know. Before we begin, I promise that I'll try never to make you feel uncomfortable about your blindness, but I won't avoid the subject either."

"You don't mince words."

She smiled. "So I've been told. Do you mind?"

He tilted his head, as though he could see beyond the bandages that covered his eyes. She remembered the piercing quality of his gaze, and for a moment she felt relieved that he couldn't see the hunger in her eyes as she studied him.

"Yes, I mind. I mind all of this."

"I don't blame you. Cyrus has a way of bulldozing people into situations. He considers his judgment calls impeccable. I guess it's up to us to make the best of a potentially awkward situation."

He chuckled, but the sound lacked any real humor.

"I'll show you to your suite now. I'm right-handed, so I generally lead off with my right foot."

Although pleased that he immediately adjusted his stride to her shorter one, Bliss didn't kid herself that Micah Holbrook was feeling cooperative. She expected resistance and anger from him in the hours and days ahead. She understood and even empathized with his inner rage, but she was nevertheless determined to draw him out of the shell he'd crawled into.

Despite the currents of tension she felt streaming through his muscular body, Bliss spoke nonchalantly. "We're entering the east wing. You've probably noticed how cool it is indoors. The floors and walls are marble. The hallway is quite long, and approximately six feet wide. There are three suites in this wing. You'll be using the one next to mine, and we'll share a patio that looks out over the back lawn and the beach. The third suite will remain vacant during your stay."

As they moved down the hallway at a sedate pace, Bliss savored the encompassing warmth of Micah's hand. She remembered when he'd been the one to watch over her, reassuring her with his presence in the London hospital, holding her hand while the doctor swabbed cuts with anesthetic and then stitched a gash to her thigh. She still bore the scar on her upper leg, now faded to a narrow white line. During those post-explosion hours, Micah had become the center of her world. She'd never forgotten him, but she realized that he hadn't ever guessed the impact he'd had on her vulnerable heart.

"There aren't any chairs or other furnishings in the hallway, so you won't have to negotiate an obstacle course when you leave your bedroom." Bliss paused in front of a closed door, brought Micah's hand to the doorknob, and said, "We're at the end of the hallway now."

He turned the knob and pushed open the door. Bliss inhaled the mingling scents of island flowers and salt-tinged Caribbean air that flowed through the open patio doors on the opposite side of the room. She took his hand and stepped forward. Micah moved with her.

"This suite is a combination sitting room and bedroom with a private bath. The furniture is contemporary, and the color scheme is a mix of creams and burgundies." She glanced at Micah and noted the muscle that ticked furiously in his already tight jaw. "I'll always describe your surroundings."

"What's the point?"

"By having mental pictures to work with, you'll get a better sense of how to move through each room."

"Are you blind?" he demanded, jerking his hand free.

"No."

"Then how the hell do you know what I need?"

"Experience. My method may not be officially sanctioned by the medical community, but it works. Cyrus trusts me," she reminded him.

He muttered a coarse word. Bliss ignored his anger, reclaimed his hand, and led him around the room. She showed him the location of each piece of furniture, the walk-in closet, and the bathroom. By forcing Micah to skim his fingertips across each surface they encountered, including the walls, she knew she was helping him imprint images in his sensory memory. She finally escorted him to the open French doors that led out to the patio.

"You can feel the breeze on your face. It's almost as good as a massage after a long day at work. It's beautiful outside today. There isn't a cloud for miles, and the temperature is in the low eighties."

"I'm tired," said Micah, turning away from a view he couldn't see. He stopped abruptly.

Bliss understood his problem. Resisting her

desire to guide him, she instead provided him with the means to deal with his disorientation himself. "There are two chairs and a coffee table approximately six feet in front of you. The low table is positioned between the chairs."

His spine as straight as an oak plank, Micah moved forward. Bliss watched him fight the urge to extend his hands in front of him, instead pressing them to his sides.

"Micah," she said quietly. He paused, his chin coming up as he tilted his head in her direction. "The leading edge of the chair cushion is about eight inches from where you're standing. Move slowly and you'll feel the presence of the chair before you actually touch it, but only if you trust your senses and let them guide you."

He moved with care and unusual grace for such a large man deprived of his sight. Once he sank into the chair, he exhaled and gripped the arms. "I didn't ask to be sent here," he announced, anger and resentment resonating in his low voice.

"I realize that."

"Why would you want a stranger in your home?"

"You're my father's friend." *And you saved my live, even though you obviously don't remember me.*

"That's not an answer."

"It's the only one I've got right now." Her gaze fell to his white-knuckled grip on the arms of the chair. She ached for him, but she kept her voice brisk as she spoke. "I'm offering you my hospitality and friendship, not pity. I save that for people who really need it."

"I don't want or need your help, and I'd like to be left alone now."

"I understand what you're saying, but I can't allow you to turn this suite into a hideout. I have some free time on my hands, and I intend to put it to good use while you're here. Cyrus told me it's uncertain if you'll regain your vision. Since your blindness could be permanent, you need to learn some good habits right off the bat."

"Get out!" he shouted, his temper finally exploding.

She approached him, her hands joined in front of her as she studied him. "You cannot deal with this situation alone, and turning yourself into a recluse until you know if the surgery's been successful or not is a mistake. You have to prepare yourself for the possibility that you'll be blind. I'm putting you on notice right now—I don't intend to let you hide from yourself or from the world. I know you're angry, but be smart enough to make your anger work for you, instead of using it against yourself."

He raked ruthless fingers through his close-cropped pale gold hair. "Please get out of here and leave me alone," he said through gritted teeth.

Bliss crossed the room. She paused at the door and looked back at Micah. She felt his panic. Trembling with diverse emotions, she lifted her chin. She knew in that instant that she would go to war with him if necessary to help him through this crisis, but she also realized she needed to remain emotionally detached.

"The evening meal is usually served at seven. I'll see you then. I hope you'll enjoy your stay at Rowland House. Cyrus calls it the perfect place for R and R. When your luggage arrives, I suggest you unpack on your own. You'll be less dependent on others if you do for yourself whatever you can."

Her heart ached for him as she watched him grapple with his rage. She thought he looked as lonely and isolated as a jagged mountain peak. While he simmered in silence, Bliss gently cautioned, "No one will be allowed to wait on you, Micah. Your rank is meaningless in my home, so don't issue any orders. Anyone who caters to you will be shipped out of here in a matter of hours."

Bliss slipped out of his suite, pulled the door closed behind her, and then sank back against it. Her hands shook, and her heart raced. Tears filled her eyes, but she angrily brushed them away. She covered her face with her hands until the sound of footsteps coming down the hall forced her to compose herself.

As she straightened and produced a smile for the young man carrying Micah's luggage, Bliss told herself she'd done the right thing by immediately establishing the ground rules for his stay. She knew she didn't have any other options with a man as strong and as stubborn as Micah Holbrook.

TWO

Micah ignored the young man who delivered his luggage, just as he ignored the passage of time. As he struggled to master the turbulent emotions rioting within him, he silently cursed Cyrus Rowland.

He remained motionless in the chair, his fists clenched and the muscles of his large body knotted with tension. He seethed with the impotent rage of a man suddenly denied control of his fate.

Micah resented the uncertainty of his situation almost as much as the thought of spending the rest of his life dependent upon others. He still couldn't endure the possibility of that kind of half-life. *He* took care of people. No one took care of him. No one.

Neither would he ever accustom himself to

being the object of pity. He preferred, he realized, the finality of death to such an existence.

A short time later, hearing footsteps on the patio, Micah recognized them immediately; but he refused to respond to Bliss's presence even when his senses alerted him to her position in the open doorway.

"The sun is about to set," she remarked as she leaned against the doorframe, her gaze captured by the natural beauty of her surroundings. "It looks like a fireball sitting on the edge of the horizon. The breeze has picked up enough to rustle the fronds of the palm trees that border the patio."

She turned away from the view and walked into his suite. "When I was a child, I'd stand out on the back lawn early in the morning, take a deep breath, and then hold it for as long as I could. I thought it was the only way to bring all the wonderful scents of the island into my body. My mother used to tell me that the fragrances of the Caribbean sweetened the heart of the person who cherished them the most." She smiled. "It made sense when I was a little, but it seems rather silly now."

Distracted from his conflicted thoughts, Micah tried to get a picture of Bliss Rowland by assembling the puzzle pieces of her unusual personality. Earlier, she'd behaved with all of the subtlety of exploding dynamite, but now he thought she sounded almost whimsical. He heard the whisper of a silky-sounding fabric flowing over her body as she moved nearer, and he felt her closeness when she paused in front of him.

The next breath he took filled his senses with her personal fragrance. He recognized it as French and very expensive, and it had a greater impact on him than he expected. He told himself that he had to be insane to be attracted to Bliss Rowland, but he felt drawn to her nonetheless. His reaction angered and baffled him, but he felt helpless to stem the tide of awareness that swept over him and saturated his senses.

"Good evening, Micah. Shall we start over?"

He turned his head away from her softly seductive voice. At that moment, feeling his loins stir, he almost hated her for making him aware of himself as a man. He dug his fingers into the arms of his chair, determined to resist her unexpected appeal. He didn't move a muscle, although he did wonder how could he want a woman he didn't know and couldn't see.

"I thought you might like to escort me to the dining room"

"I'm not hungry."

"That's hard to believe. The cook told me you haven't eaten since early this morning."

"Leave me the hell alone," he ordered.

"You already know I can't do that, Micah."

She sank to her knees between his muscular thighs. He told himself he didn't want her to touch him, and yet he craved her closeness because it meant a temporary reprieve from the physical isolation he'd experienced since his surgery. Why did she understand, he wondered resentfully, that he needed human contact right now?

"You have every right to be angry with Cyrus," she said, jarring him as she voiced his earlier thoughts. "He's incredibly high-handed, but I think we both know him well enough to realize that he took control of your life only because he believed you'd lost it. You also have every right to be annoyed with me, especially after our conversation this afternoon. I provoked you in order to get your attention. My purpose wasn't to hurt you."

He felt the strength in her slender hands when she forced open his fists and flattened her palms over his. He seized her wrists, unable to keep himself from treating her like a lifeline even though he loathed the need within himself.

"You have to make a decision, Micah. Either this is going to be a battle of wills, or you're going to cooperate with me."

"I've made my decision, so you can leave now."

"Try again," she challenged gently.

"Don't badger me."

"Since I have no intention of coddling you, I guess you're stuck with badgering. Micah, listen to me, please. We can't risk catering to you or babying you. Cyrus is worried about you. He sent you here because he trusts me, not because he was trying to punish you. He thinks you're important. So do I."

"You don't even know me," he responded, his scorn apparent.

"I know about you. I know you can't use the telephone or a computer keyboard right now. I know you're apprehensive about eating a meal in front of people, just as I know everything you can't see makes you feel as though you're moving through a mine field each time you take a step. I know you're angry that others are making the simplest decisions for you, like what you'll wear each morning or how you'll spend your day. I know you can't read the newspaper or a book. I also know you feel trapped and isolated, and you're starting to think you'd be better off dead, because the alternative is to become a burden to your loved ones. What's happened to you would disorient the strongest, most secure person in the world." She paused, giving him a moment to digest her comments, and then asked softly, "Don't I know enough, Micah?" Pulling free of his grip, Bliss started to get to her feet.

Shaken by her intuition of his most pressing fears and by his anxiety over what his life might be like if he didn't regain his vision, Micah responded instinctively. He reached out with lightning quickness, connected with her shoulders, and grabbed hold of her. Pulling her forward, he hauled her up and into his lap. She weighed almost nothing, he realized in surprise. She also didn't protest his aggressive behavior, which surprised him even more.

Her compassionate voice continued to echo in his head as he spanned her waist with his hands and held her atop his thighs. He trembled with tension and a startling renewal of the desire he'd felt just minutes earlier, and he realized somewhat belatedly that Bliss wasn't fighting to free herself.

Micah frowned when he noticed that her breathing hadn't even changed. Did nothing shake this woman? Why wasn't she upset with him? Why wasn't she fighting him like a wildcat? Did she think the bandages covering his eyes made him less of a man? He assumed the latter, and anger reignited within him.

"Now what?" she finally asked, her calm voice like salt applied to an open wound.

Micah's grip on her waist tightened. He wanted her to struggle against his hold, but she didn't, damn her! He exhaled, the sound ragged with emotions he couldn't even begin to articulate.

What *did* he want from her?

Aside from the driving need to touch her, to reassure himself that she was more than a voice capable of irritating the hell out of him as she relentlessly peeled back his anxieties layer by layer, he finally admitted to himself that he'd reached a point where he just wanted a temporary peace. But he didn't want her pity. He particularly didn't want Bliss Rowland's pity.

She reached for his sunglasses, eased them off his face, and tossed them onto the coffee table. Micah stiffened, wary because he couldn't quite figure out her motives, but he didn't try to stop her. His ego protested because she could now see the bandages that covered his eyes, but he knew she wasn't trying to harm or humiliate him. Nevertheless, he felt vulnerable without the protection of his sunglasses.

Micah also felt every subtle movement of her body. He grudgingly gave her credit for not squirming in his lap, but her innocent movements nevertheless enticed and aroused a body that had gone without the pleasure of physical intimacy for a very long time. Desire streamed hotly through his veins, and he shifted beneath her, seeking to ease the pressure in his loins without revealing his need.

Bliss placed her hands on his broad shoulders. He stiffened instantly, on guard lest she should touch his face.

"Relax, Micah."

He realized again that she didn't feel the least bit threatened by his anger or his physical response to her. Still unsure why she'd allowed him to manhandle her right into his lap, he waited warily for her next move.

Bliss skimmed her hands over his shoulders and up the sides of his neck. Micah experienced a reluctant kind of appreciation when he felt her unexpectedly capable touch as she massaged the knotted muscles beneath her fingertips, but he refused to voice his feelings.

Letting his mind drift, Micah started to relax. But a short while later he felt the sting of betrayal as Bliss raised her hands to the sides of his face and pressed her palms to his cheeks. He grabbed her wrists, but her whispered "Please, Micah" made him hesitate.

Lowering his hands, he felt her press her fingertips to his temples and move them in a circular motion. Her touch, gentle, firm, and incredibly effective, seduced Micah in ways he'd never imagined possible. His world, a world of subterfuge and violence, hadn't prepared him for a woman like Bliss Rowland. Whatever her agenda, his senses responded to her wholeheartedly. He wanted—*needed*—to believe, if only for the present, that she was as sincere and caring as her touch implied. Moments later, the headache throbbing in his temples started to ease.

Although grateful for her kindness and the soothing quality of her fingertips, Micah still felt the ravages of his inner war. He knew that not all Bliss's compassion and sensitivity would ever quell his emotional conflicts or the fears that haunted him.

He still felt the urge to ram his fist through the nearest wall, to shout his rage at the car bomb that had altered his life less than a month ago. His headache started to return, and he bit back a groan.

Bliss withdrew her hands without warning. "I'm going to stand up now, Micah. I want you to stand with me."

He didn't try to restrain her as she scrambled out of his lap, but he regretted her absence almost immediately. He told himself that because she seemed willing to understand and accept his constantly shifting emotions, he could afford to reward her by cooperating with her. Although he got to his feet, Micah didn't move away from his chair.

Bliss took his hands. He sensed that she was asking for his trust, but he'd never given trust easily. He knew it empowered the recipient,

and power could be misused by even the most
well-intentioned person.

"You need to see me, and this is the best
way," Bliss said.

She brought his open palms to her face and
pressed them to her cheeks. More curious
about her than he wanted to admit, Micah
hesitated briefly before cupping her head and
tunneling his fingers into the soft curls that
framed her face.

"You're not very tall."

She laughed, then teased, "Don't let the
size of the package fool you."

"Are you telling me you're tougher than
you . . . look?" He spat the last word. Micah
didn't see her smile fade, but he felt her sudden
stillness. Would he ever be able to simply *look* at
a woman? he wondered. Would he ever again
see the naked body of a lover or view the satisfaction that glazed a woman's eyes in the after-
math of passion? His hold on Bliss tightened as
he questioned whether he'd ever even have
another lover.

"Touch me, Micah," she encouraged, her
voice steady, her manner serene, despite the
fierceness of his expression and the tension in
his hands. "See me with your fingertips. Create
an image in your mind to go along with what
your senses have already told you about me. *Use*
your senses, Micah. Use the gifts God gave you

to recognize the face of a friend, because that's exactly what I am."

Unease tremored through him, followed by a sudden burst of desire. His hands shook as hers dropped away, and she lifted her face for his inspection. Micah felt clumsy as he pressed his fingertips to her forehead.

He discovered smooth skin stretched tautly over a high forehead. Nervousness gave way to a concentration that those few who knew Micah Holbrook well would have expected of him. As he breathed deeply of Bliss's unique scent, Micah shifted his fingertips to her temples and discovered throbbing pulse points with the callused pads of his fingers.

As he slowly brought his thumbs across her arched eyebrows, he sensed a delicacy in her features that seemed at odds with her assertive personality. He moved lower, his fingers fanning her hairline as he carefully stroked his thumbs over her closed eyes. Dense lashes that reminded him of mink feathered over his skin and sent sensation after sensation shimmering across his nerve endings.

"Talk to me," he said, his voice almost loverlike as he traced the shape of her slender nose and the elegance of her high cheekbones.

"My skin is very fair, but I tan easily. My eyes are blue, and my hair is as black as ink. I've been told that I resemble my mother."

Cupping the side of her face with his broad-palmed hand, Micah trailed a fingertip across the seam of her lips, then back over the lush fullness of her lower lip. Her mouth invited a leisurely exploration, and his body tightened in response to that invitation.

He felt her tremble, and then he heard her breath catch. He froze, certain she felt uncomfortable with his touch despite her earlier encouragement. "What's wrong?"

"Nothing."

Frowning, he asked, "Would you rather I didn't touch you?"

"No, I'm fine." He felt Bliss place her hands over his as though to emphasize that she spoke the truth. "As you touch me, think about the sensory bridge that exists between the sighted world and the unsighted world," she suggested quietly. "We both know there's a seventy percent chance you'll be visually impaired, so you need to give some thought to constructing that bridge yourself—it's the only way you'll ever be comfortable when you travel it."

Micah didn't want to hear about the risk he faced. He needed to concentrate on Bliss, not on himself, so he focused for several silent moments on the shape of her generous mouth and the images that filled his mind and tantalized his senses. His entire body throbbed with desire, and his male instincts told him that making love with this woman would be like her name—bliss.

Micah exhaled shakily and forced his thoughts away from the sensual hunger that tantalized him. "You aren't telling me anything I haven't already figured out for myself," he finally admitted a few moments later.

"Do you intend to build that bridge, Micah?" she asked, a hint of urgency in her voice. "Do you believe you're capable of building it? Do you really understand that your mind, your heart, and your will to succeed are separate parts of your being, and that they aren't dependent on your vision?"

He knew what she wanted him to say, but he couldn't say it. He didn't know the true answer to her questions yet, so he remained silent and continued his exploration of her features, feeling her disappointment in the rush of air that escaped her when she sighed.

He trailed his knuckles across the width of her lower lip, simultaneously fascinated and tempted by the soft flesh and the warmth of her breath. He craved a very thorough taste of Bliss Rowland, but he consciously fought the urge to stake a claim on her by reminding himself that she hadn't granted him any rights beyond her offer of friendship.

"I don't understand anything right now,"

he muttered more to himself than to her. Anger resonated in his voice. Driving his fingers into the cap of silky curls that covered her head and framed her face, he kneaded her scalp like a jungle cat fondling its prey.

Bliss suddenly slipped free of him. Micah's head came up. He reached out, made contact with her shoulders, and seized her.

"Very good. See what happens when you trust your instincts?"

He scowled. "I don't like tests."

"Neither do I, so there won't be any more."

"You're very small, aren't you?"

"And you're quite large," she countered.

"Not for my family." Turmoil stirred within him yet again. How in God's name, he wondered, would he tell his parents that he might never see again? Hating the thought, he let his shoulders slump.

"I'm five feet three inches tall," Bliss said hurriedly. "I weigh a hundred and ten pounds. I'm single, twenty-eight, and I have all my teeth."

He realized that she'd noticed his anxiety and was making an effort to distract him from it. He wondered yet again why she even cared about his state of mind. "Am I supposed to count them now?" he asked, referring to her teeth.

"Only if you absolutely have to," she teased, despite his obvious sarcasm.

He smiled, his first genuine smile since his arrival, and tangled his fingers in the tumbled curls that partially covered her nape. "It's soft."

"My hairdresser thanks you."

Concentrating, he shifted his hands and curved them over her shoulders. He recognized the fabric. "Raw silk."

"That's right. What do you hear in my voice?"

He hesitated for a moment. "Approval?"

"What does that suggest to you?"

"You tell me," he answered, although he took her point.

"You have to listen to the words and emotions in the voices you listen to. Most people don't realize that they reveal their feelings when they speak. Since you won't always have the luxury of physical contact, what you hear is doubly important."

"Your perfume is French, which also proves that my nose works. What of it?" He refused to care if his sarcasm offended her.

"Your senses need to work in concert, but you have to allow them the opportunity. For the record that particular fragrance is my only vice."

"And here I thought you were perfect."

Micah slid his large hands down her arms, measured her narrow wrists with his fingers, and then clasped her hands. He felt the flexing strength of her fingers when she squeezed his hands. "You're remarkably petite."

"So you keep saying."

"A man could hurt you very easily."

"You won't."

He heard the conviction in her voice. Although pleased that she didn't perceive him as abusive, he wasn't certain he liked being so transparent. "How can you be sure? You don't know me."

"Your hands. They say a lot about you."

"Like what?"

"You're aware of your physical prowess. When you aren't feeling angry or threatened, your touch is very light." Bliss paused. "The real question is whether or not you'll accept my compassion and assistance at this difficult time in your life. It's a new role for you, I suspect."

"What in hell did Cyrus tell you about me?" he demanded, thrown by yet another of his hostess's blunt curves.

"Enough for me to realize that you're always in the driver's seat in every relationship you have. And enough to understand that you instinctively balk at the idea of depending on anyone other than yourself in a crisis."

"You're lying," he accused. "Cyrus wouldn't have said those things."

"It's what he didn't say that was so revealing," she admitted.

"You're spooky, lady. Very spooky."

"No, I'm just me, and I never apologize for being myself. Do you?" Bliss challenged him.

"Hell, no!"

"Then we're standing on a level playing field, aren't we?" When he didn't answer, she filled the silence. "I can't force you to do anything you don't want to do, Micah."

"You'll just talk me to death, is that it?" he retorted.

Bliss laughed. "Probably," she conceded.

He discovered that he liked the sound of her laughter. It was warm and rich, hinting at a vitality of spirit that he suddenly envied. Almost without thought, he released her hands and lifted his fingertips to the edges of her lips.

Making out the shape of her lingering smile, Micah felt a sudden burst of apprehension. He didn't want to like anything about Bliss Rowland. He already desired her with a hunger he hadn't felt for any woman in years, and that was bad enough. He also feared becoming her personal cause, a charity case she felt compelled to adopt because of his connection to her father. He feared as well becoming dependent on her.

"Micah . . ."

"I don't want to like you," he said bluntly, his hands falling to his sides before he lowered himself back into the chair. His frustration with the situation doused his desire like a bucket of water poured over a campfire. "And I'll be damned if I'll depend on you. I don't need a nursemaid."

Bliss walked around to stand behind his chair. She soothed him by massaging his rigid shoulders. "Of course you don't want to like me. It's risky, because if you like me, you'll have to trust me."

"Why?" he demanded. "Why do this? Why become involved in my life? Why put yourself through this? You don't owe me anything."

"And I don't pity you either," she snapped.

He grabbed her wrists, trapping her and forcing her to hover at an odd angle behind him. "Everyone has an agenda, Bliss Rowland. What's yours?"

He interpreted her sigh as a sign of patience stretched to the limit and felt a perverse need to push her until he found her breaking point.

"Do you assign motives to every person you meet?" she asked.

"Absolutely. In my business it's the only way to stay alive."

"You are a man of character, strength, and

purpose, Micah Holbrook, which is why your work in Naval Intelligence is respected by men like my father. And your success or failure in your current situation is largely dependent on your willingness to accept a challenge."

"Now you sound like him," said Micah, his voice gravel rough.

Bliss flinched. Micah felt the sharp movement as it jarred her slender frame.

"I just want to help you," she said softly.

He jerked on her wrists. "Try again."

"You're hurting me."

Stung by her comment, he instantly freed her.

She straightened and moved to his side. "The household staff has instructions not to deliver any meal trays to your suite without my permission. You have three options. Come with me now, find the kitchen yourself, or go hungry. It's your choice."

"Nice! Real nice!" he shouted.

She slipped a circular object, heavy and cool to the touch, into his open palm. Micah closed his hand around it, his curiosity roused despite his frustration.

"You're holding a pocket watch. Press the stem at the top to open it. It needs to be re-wound once a day."

"Damn you! I . . . cannot . . . see." He ground out the words through clenched teeth.

"Don't be obtuse, Micah. It doesn't suit you." Bliss walked away, but she paused in the doorway to the patio. "Last chance for the evening meal."

He sat as still and silent as a stone mountain until she slipped out of his suite. Only then did Micah open the watch and smooth his fingertip across the face. For the first time in weeks he knew the exact time.

THREE

Bliss hated losing her temper, and now she sternly reminded herself that Micah's needs took precedence over her own inner emotional turmoil. Although she ate a solitary meal in the dining room and spent the remainder of the evening in her studio, she continued to feel his presence.

She chided herself several times that she had to get beyond the magnetism storming her senses, but she suspected she was destined to a tightrope existence for the duration of their time together. She seriously doubted that her heart would allow her to ignore the feelings Micah evoked in her.

Although still restless and on edge, Bliss returned to her suite well after midnight. As she showered and dressed for bed, she realized how easy it would be for her to fall in love with Micah again. But she would risk far more as a grown woman than she'd risked as a teenager in the throes of her first crush. She realized, too, that secret dreams and private yearnings wouldn't satisfy her this time. She would want more, need more, if Micah responded to her.

Afraid of her vulnerability, Bliss absently studied her reflection in the bathroom mirror. She saw eyes shadowed by fatigue and haunted by memories of abandonment by people she'd trusted. Her chin trembled until she clenched her teeth and glared at her image, proclaiming herself a fool for wanting a man she couldn't have.

Emotions submerged for many years beneath an independent life-style, inherited wealth, creative success far beyond anything she'd ever anticipated, and her hunger to be loved without motive strained to burst free. Bliss swore, the sound a hushed whisper in the silence of the night.

Turning off the light, she walked into her bedroom. Moonlight spilled through the open patio doors and across the marble floor. Hearing footsteps, Bliss paused halfway to her bed, detouring to the open French doors that led out onto the patio.

It was probably one of the security guards checking on Micah, she told herself, even as she felt compelled to make sure. She hesitated when she recognized the man pacing the patio. Smiling, she experienced a moment of pure pride. Micah had left the safety of his suite. Although he hadn't gone far, Bliss considered his presence on the moon-washed patio a positive sign: He'd grown tired of hiding.

His ability to navigate the patio without hesitation told her that he'd carefully inspected the area, discovering in the process the placement of a few pieces of wicker furniture as well as the flower beds and palm trees that bordered it. She said a quiet prayer that he would one day be able to enjoy the view of the back lawn, the beach, and the turquoise beauty of the Caribbean waters, but until then, Bliss silently promised herself, she would teach him to maximize his other senses. Even if he wound up hating her for her efforts.

Standing in the doorway, she waited in silence as the night breeze ruffled the hem of her white silk nightgown. Micah paused less than a minute later, his head lifting as he turned in her direction. Wearing the same clothes he'd traveled in, he looked bone-weary and rumpled.

Bliss moved on bare feet across the patio. Aware of the importance of indicating her exact location at all times in order not to disorient him, she remarked, "You've had a long day. I'm surprised you aren't asleep."

"I'd like to be left alone." Micah turned, extended his hand, and moved toward the double doors to his suite.

"I witnessed what happened to my mother when she lost her vision a few years before her death. She was a diabetic all her life. She coped really well with many of the limitations her illness imposed on her, but when her vision started to fail, she grew frightened and angry."

He stopped suddenly. "Is that what you think of me?" Micah demanded. "That I'm frightened and angry?"

Bliss knew better than to answer his question. "Mother shut herself away from the world. She stopped traveling, she refused to socialize with her friends, and she quit inviting people into our home. I was a senior in college at the time. When she didn't attend my graduation ceremony, I knew something was terribly wrong, so I came home. She'd kept the truth from me for several months, and the servants had honored her instructions that I not be informed of her situation."

She sighed, the memories coming back full force as she walked to the edge of the patio and looked at the stars that studded the night sky like diamond chips. "I did and said everything I could think of to persuade her she was strong enough to handle what was happening to her. Mother fought me tooth and nail, and it took months, but I finally reached her. In the end she fought the battle of her life, and along the way we learned what she needed to do to compensate for her vision loss. We did it together, Micah. And Cyrus sent you to me because he knows I've never forgotten what she went through."

Micah turned slowly. He moved forward with care, but without hesitation. "I've known Cyrus Rowland for a long time. He's never even mentioned your mother to me."

"He wouldn't. If you think about it, you'll recall that he never discusses his personal life with anyone. They divorced when I was five, and they rarely saw each other after that."

"So you lived with her?"

"That's right."

"Here?"

"Part of the time. I attended schools in Switzerland and England while I was growing up. Mother kept apartments in Zurich and just outside London. I enjoyed traveling with her during summer vacations and other holidays—I didn't realize that her restlessness was caused by loneliness and her fear of premature death."

Micah stood beside her. "You don't like to travel so much anymore, do you?"

His insight pleased her. "Not at all. Other than a periodic trip to see friends, I stay rooted. I'm a nester at heart, and I really love Saint

Thomas." Bliss inhaled deeply of the fragrant humid air currents that flowed over her before turning to study Micah's profile. "What about you? Is there a place you particularly like, a place that gives you a sense of belonging whenever you're there?"

"I used to feel that way about the Pacific Northwest, but that was a long time ago. I've lived a pretty transient life since the Naval Academy. In my line of work you learn not to form any permanent ties to people or places."

Shifting sideways, Micah extended his hands. As he reached for Bliss, his knuckles brushed across the silk-covered tips of her breasts.

She inhaled sharply, the whispery contact paralyzing her senses for a moment. She felt Micah's surprise, saw the shocked stillness of his body as she stared up at him. It occurred to her that the angles and hollows of his hard-featured face appeared even more forbidding than usual.

She managed a steadying breath, aware that she had to distance herself from him even as her nipples beaded with tension and her senses produced an image of his mouth at her breasts, his tongue and lips subjecting her to a glorious sensual torture. But she couldn't seem to move, didn't want to move, despite the frantic voice in

her head that shouted one warning after another.

"You're wearing silk again."

"Yes," she whispered breathlessly, mes-
merized by the feel of his fingertips as he traced
the piping on the bodice of her nightgown. She
shivered, despite the heat of his fingertips as he
trailed them over the upper slopes of her full
breasts.

"And lace?"

"Yes," she said, her voice growing even
fainter when he briefly dipped a fingertip into
the valley between her breasts.

"I seem to need to touch you when we're
together."

She heard his bafflement and sensed his
growing confusion. She also felt the tremor
that shook him when he smoothed his fingertips over the warm skin above her breasts. After
fingering the pulse that throbbed in the hollow
of her throat, he curved his hands over her
shoulders.

Bliss breathed shallowly. Her insides
churned, and her heart raced. She understood
the reassurance he found in physical contact,
but she also felt fear stir in her own heart that
she might weaken in the face of his need and
allow him to use her.

Micah ran his hands down her arms, then
shifted them to span her waist. His thumbs

smoothed over and up her midriff, then stroked the undersides of her breasts. She felt them swell in anticipation of his touch. Sensation cascaded through her. Her legs turned rubbery, and she bit back the plea for greater intimacy that hovered on the tip of her tongue. As he dragged his knuckles down across her stomach and then cupped her hips, she felt his hands shake as he urged her closer.

She swayed against him, nearly shattered by the desire streaming through her even as she registered the strength of his body's response to her. Gripping his forearms, Bliss struggled to maintain her equilibrium despite Micah's obvious need to reassure himself that he was still capable of arousing a woman.

Suddenly she trembled so violently that he released her. He closed his hands into fists and lifted his chin in a gesture of defense that Bliss recognized.

"Are you afraid of me?"

"Of course not," she insisted. "I feel a lot of things when you touch me, but fear isn't one of them."

"You're remarkably blunt for a woman," he noted. "What are you thinking right now?"

"That I'm glad you're here."

He raised a hand to the strand of dark gold hair that had fallen across his forehead and shoved at it with ruthless fingers. "Why?"

Bliss almost smiled at the incredulous tone of his voice. "Because I like you."

"You hardly know me. Do you always let men you don't know touch you so intimately?"

She stiffened but controlled her temper. "I trust my instincts, Micah. You don't intend to harm me or to use me. You're simply testing the boundaries of our relationship, which isn't all that surprising, given your situation."

"You're real big on instinct, aren't you?"

"You needn't sound so cynical. I trust my instincts because they're usually right. And I suspect you've stayed alive over the years by doing exactly the same thing."

"What do your instincts tell you about me?"

She hedged. "It's difficult to put it all into words."

"Try." He jerked her forward, aligning their lower bodies with an ease that startled Bliss. She felt his fingers dig into her hips as he forced her to feel his reaction to her.

Bliss sensed it would be a mistake to put her instincts about him into words. "You're trying to make me angry, but it won't work."

"Are you sure?" He rubbed against her, and a low groan escaped him. "You feel like a sin-filled version of heaven."

"Micah." In saying his name, she voiced a clear warning.

He stilled his hips but failed to conceal the shudder that rumbled through his taut body. Bliss felt tension arc between them like an electrical current. She craved his passion, but she also needed his trust, and she knew she would lose it if she allowed their relationship to become intimate.

"We shouldn't complicate an already complicated situation, should we?" she asked.

"Is there a man in your life?"

"No."

"Why not?"

"I don't trust easily, and I dislike being used," she explained, deliberately allowing him to think she suspected him of using her to slake his sexual hunger.

"You've been used?" A wary stillness seemed to overtake him.

"Yes, but only once. It won't happen again."

His grip on her hips eased. When she shifted backward, he didn't try to stop her. "You sound very determined right now. You also sound like another woman I know." He paused. "Leah, my baby sister."

"I'm determined not to be hurt." Having resented the mention of another woman, then feeling immediate relief at his explanation of who she was, Bliss shrugged beneath the hands he curved over her shoulders. Act as though you're indifferent, she told herself. After all, he's a virile man, and he's probably had lovers by the dozens. But the very thought of another woman in his arms made her queasy. "I like my life, Micah. It's very full and satisfying, and I don't need any complications. Neither do you, for that matter."

"We have something in common, or we did until about a month ago."

Bliss didn't object when he tugged her into a loose embrace. Although surprised that he held her with an absence of overt desire, she welcomed the haven she found in his arms. She slid her hands around his waist and laced her fingers together. "Your career means everything to you, doesn't it?"

"It's how I've always defined myself."

"I think people define themselves and then adapt their instincts and personalities to the work they choose to do."

"Interesting concept, but there's something missing from your theory."

"What do you mean?"

"Who in hell's going to trust a blind man?" he demanded. "I've worked in Naval Intelligence for most of my adult life. It's what I know, and it's what I'm good at."

She hurt for him, but she knew if she acknowledged her feelings, Micah would interpret her response as pity. Bliss lifted her head from his shoulder. "If the surgery isn't a success and you don't regain your sight, some people will lose confidence in you. Others may become overprotective. Those reactions go with the territory, I'm afraid. There will also be people who will trust you, but only if you make it happen. You have to set the tone, Micah. If you expect pity, you'll get it in spades. But if you expect to be treated normally and then behave accordingly, people will respond to your cues."

"You really believe all that, don't you?"

"Yes," she whispered, her gaze skimming the strong lines of his jaw and the sensuality of his mouth. Pressing her hands to his muscular chest, she absorbed through her fingers and palms the warmth of his skin despite the shirt he wore. "Promise me you won't give up on yourself."

He took her hands, lifted them to his lips, and then pressed a kiss into the center of each palm. "I can't promise you anything right now, Bliss Rowland."

She sagged a little as he released her and stepped backward. "I understand." She really did understand, she realized as she instinctively closed her hands into fists to hold the heat left by his lips. A promise on his part meant a commitment Micah wouldn't break. Despite her disappointment, Bliss respected his honesty.

"I wish I did," he admitted, his voice bleak.

"Try to be optimistic about the surgery."

"Shall I hope for the best, like a good little scout?"

She stiffened, anger bursting to life inside her. "Perhaps you should, but first get rid of that chip on your shoulder. It isn't an attractive addition to your wardrobe." She stepped away from him, still smarting from his sarcasm. "I need some sleep. So do you."

"I need a lot of things."

Bliss paused in the doorway to her suite. She glanced back at Micah, taking a moment to strengthen her resolve to do what was right for him. "I know you feel as though you're riding an out-of-control roller coaster right now, but I can't let you use me simply because I'm convenient. I'm offering you my friendship, Micah, but nothing more."

"*That* I understand," he retorted bitterly.

She didn't correct him. She knew he'd be better off if he believed that she wasn't attracted to him, just as she knew that the feverish desire she felt for him would probably never fade. Feeling torn in two, she gripped the doorframe and quelled the urge to comfort him with the tenderness, love, and passion that she normally channeled into her sculpting. She even managed to speak in a level, unemotional voice. "Dr. Chalmers will arrive midmorning for your checkup. He's a retired surgeon, and he's been asked by the Department of the Navy to supervise your medical needs while you're here."

Micah flinched, but he said nothing as she stepped into her suite and quietly secured the French doors. A violent word hurtled past his lips before he could stop it. He made his way into the bedroom, slamming the doors so hard that he half expected the glass to shatter. He told himself that he didn't care if the entire building fell down around his ears.

He moved through the dark room, his rage making him careless. He cursed yet again when he walked into an armoire positioned near the bed. He finally found the bed and jerked back the spread. After shoving all but one of the pillows onto the floor, he kicked off his deck shoes and shed his clothes. Finally he stretched out atop the mattress, his naked body rigid with tension, his mind filled with the images of a sensuous woman welcoming him into her heart and body.

The woman, delicate, dark-haired, and as willful as any female he'd ever known, was Bliss Rowland. It didn't matter that he couldn't see her—he nevertheless couldn't banish the erotic images forming in his mind.

Micah listened to the sound of his own harsh breathing. He resented the desire that fired his blood, and the woman who seemed determined to challenge him on every imaginable level.

Made vulnerable by the arousal pummeling his senses, Micah reminded himself that no woman in her right mind would saddle herself with half a man, let alone invite him into her bed. But Bliss continued to haunt his thoughts.

He realized that she aroused far more than mere physical hunger in him. She inspired the unsuspected need for something deeper than the casual affairs he usually conducted with women of the world. Dalliances with any other kind of woman, he'd decided long ago, were a mistake.

A man dedicated to avoiding emotional commitment, primarily because of the dangers posed by his covert work for Naval Intelligence, Micah sensed that Bliss possessed the potential to become a pivotal person in his world, but he felt reluctant to grant her that kind of power over him. He also cursed Cyrus Rowland for forcing him out of the hospital and into an unknown environment. One day, he silently vowed, he would confront the older man and make it clear that he resented Cyrus's machinations.

Micah found little relief once he finally fell

asleep. He tossed and turned until dawn, his subconscious alternating between fantasies that featured a sensual creature named Bliss and the explosion that had nearly killed Cyrus and several other foreign dignitaries attending a multinational conference in Central America.

Micah abandoned his bed around dawn. His mood dark, he clumsily showered and dressed, then retreated to the chair in the sitting room. When he heard activity beyond the walls of his bedroom, he waited with growing impatience and an empty stomach for one of the security-team members to check on him. He intended to order a breakfast tray, and he promised himself that he'd get one, with or without Bliss Rowland's approval.

Bliss waited in the hallway while Dr. Chalmers examined Micah and changed the dressings covering his eyes. Clad in a pair of shorts, a loose top, and sandals, she looked more rested than she actually felt. She smiled when the retired physician pulled open the door.

"We're all done, Bliss. Your houseguest, I'm afraid, is a reluctant patient."

Bliss followed the white-haired surgeon into the suite. Her gaze went immediately to Micah. She noticed the muscle ticking in his unshaven jaw, as well as his white-knuckled fists. She also took in the gray T-shirt and shorts he wore, a spark of pleasure bursting to life inside her because she realized that he'd opted to explore the contents of his suitcase without help. It was a small victory, she knew, but a victory nonetheless.

His attire did nothing to conceal the brawny power of his muscular body, and his conservatively cut golden hair looked as though he'd shoved his fingers through it after stepping out of the shower. He reminded her yet again of a bold Viking adventurer. Her heartbeat accelerated, but she quickly put the brakes on her response to Micah and reminded herself to remain aloof.

"You're a fortunate man, Micah," observed the doctor as he closed his medical bag.

"Why's that?" Micah snapped.

Dr. Chalmers ignored his ill humor. "Our Bliss is an old hand with the visually impaired, and she's our principal fund-raiser for the island's residential school for the blind, which is named for her mother. She's also beautiful, talented, and remarkably even-tempered."

"Yeah, Doc. She's a regular saint! I'll tell you a secret about 'our Bliss.' She's heavily into torture and starvation."

Dr. Chalmers chuckled as he glanced at Bliss. She fought the flush staining her cheeks, then shrugged helplessly. She accepted an affectionate hug and a thumbs-up gesture from the doctor, then watched him collect his medical bag and pause beside Micah's chair.

"I don't expect a salute or a thank-you, son, but I do expect the courtesy of a handshake."

Micah shot to his feet and extended his hand. Dr. Chalmers accepted it with his usual graciousness. Bliss knew he hadn't deliberately tried to embarrass Micah. Rather, he'd reminded him that good manners were not the prerogative of the sighted alone.

"Bliss is an extraordinarily resourceful woman. Once you get past the self-pity you're feeling, you'll recognize how fortunate you are."

She watched Micah go rigid with anger and decided to intervene. "Dr. Chalmers is somewhat prejudiced, Micah. He's my godfather."

"I also delivered you, young lady. Of course I'm prejudiced." Glancing at his patient before he strolled out of the room, he said, "I'll see you both the day after tomorrow. If you need anything in the interim, Bliss knows how to reach me."

Once the doctor departed, Micah announced, "I'm hungry. I want a breakfast tray. Now."

"Brunch will be served in the dining room in about twenty minutes."

"Forget it. I'll eat in here."

"I'll meet you in the foyer at the end of the hallway. Count your steps as you make your way down the hall and remember the number. You'll have an easier time making your way around the mansion if you measure the rooms and hallways with your footsteps."

Micah moved toward her. Bliss didn't budge. That he seemed to know her exact location, which meant he was paying close attention to the sound of her voice, displaced any uneasiness she might otherwise have felt.

"I will not be trained to perform like some blasted circus animal!"

She felt something snap deep inside herself. "Stop snarling at me, Micah. I'm tired of it. You have to live your life. I'll show you how. Now you've got ten minutes to find your way to the foyer. Shoes are optional around here."

She turned away from him, tears stinging her eyes. She grasped his anxiety and longed to console him, but she knew better. Blinking back her tears, Bliss lifted her chin, a stubborn look on her face as she glanced back over her shoulder at him.

Micah seemed stunned by her remarks, and Bliss felt like the cruelest thing on two feet. But she remained determined to get him out of his suite.

As he clenched his fists at his sides and

breathed shallowly, Bliss quietly goaded him: "I'd hate to think you're a coward, Micah Holbrook."

She hurriedly exited the room, but not because she feared a violent response from Micah. She knew he simply needed to calm down sufficiently to consider his options.

Cooperation or hunger.

FOUR

Coward?

The word sounded and felt like a gun fired at point-blank range. It rang in his ears, until he managed to clamp down on his reverberating emotions.

Coward?

He didn't want to believe that Bliss Rowland thought him a coward, but she obviously did. Too stunned to move, Micah vibrated with a primitive inner fury that made him crave revenge. He pressed his clenched fists to his sides, breathing deeply as he struggled to calm himself and think in a clearheaded manner.

His pride finally kicked in, but it took a few minutes. Micah knew he had no choice but to pick up the guantlet Bliss had tossed at his feet. She held all the cards at the moment, but he silently vowed that he would beat her at her own game. He also promised himself that he would find a way to make her feel as raw-nerved and vulnerable as she'd made him feel.

With the word "coward" still ricocheting through his consciousness, he marshaled his emotions, walked to the bedroom door, and jerked it open. Micah didn't intend to go hungry any longer. He also didn't intend to allow a woman he barely knew to judge him.

Squaring his broad shoulders, he forced himself to concentrate. He stepped out of the suite, touched the wall to his right in order to get his bearings, and made his way down the hallway. He counted every step he took.

Micah settled down as he walked. He felt the subtly shifting air currents in the hallway and heard the faint hum of a motor—caused, he assumed, by overhead fans. As he approached the foyer, he started to experience a sensation of expanded space. He slowed his steps, but he kept counting. When he ran out of wall, he paused.

"You're doing fine, Micah."

He stepped forward, using her voice as an auditory beacon. Although still furious with Bliss, Micah allowed his pride and his senses to guide him toward her.

"I'm directly in front of you," she said. "I think you'll like the meal I've arranged for us."

Micah detected her fragrance, took a final step, and paused. Extending his hands, he found her shoulders with ease. He gripped them, his fingers a conduit for the tension coursing through his entire body. He expected a reaction, wanted one even, but she failed to supply one.

Annoyed, Micah deliberately ran his fingertips down her arms, his senses alert to any telltale sign of apprehension on her part. She seemed unmoved by his nearness and his touch as he traced the inside curves of her wrists. Micah suddenly realized that she expected him to behave aggressively, and he regretted giving her what she wanted.

"If you're angry with me, Micah, say so. I don't read minds."

"Quit trying to manipulate me. It won't work."

"I did what I had to do."

"I don't like your tactics, lady."

"Then don't force me to use them again," she suggested, her tone supremely reasonable.

He slid his fingers up her inner arms, pausing finally at the hemmed sleeves of the top she wore. "What have you got on?"

"White shorts and shirt."

"Cotton?" he speculated as he fingered the fabric, determined to keep her off balance until he could figure her out. While he thought

about what it would feel like to conduct a leisurely exploration of the curves and hollows of
her naked body with his fingertips, he contented himself with inhaling the alluring scent
of her skin.

"That's right."

He trailed his fingers down over her narrow
wrists and then across the backs of her hands.
He felt a faint tremor run through her and
wondered if he made her nervous. He hoped
so. He sincerely hoped so. As they stood there,
he cursed the darkness that prevented him from
seeing her face, from reading the emotion in
her eyes.

Bliss suddenly pulled free of him, clasped
one of his hands, and turned so that they stood
side by side. "Let's go into the dining room."

He didn't budge. "Your skin's very soft."

She laughed—uneasily, to Micah's ears. "I
haven't got time for a beauty regimen, so the
humid climate gets all the credit."

"You washed your hair this morning." He
felt her surprise, not just the shift in her stance
when she glanced at him. Micah intended to
prove to her that he wasn't as dull-witted as she
apparently assumed.

"How did you know?"

"I can smell your shampoo."

"Good for you."

Micah shrugged to make it clear that her

praise meant nothing, then matched his footsteps to her shorter stride as they walked across the foyer. His dignity felt a little less damaged now, and that realization gave him confidence.

Bliss slowed her pace and cautioned, "Two steps down, Micah. All the floors and walls in the mansion are white marble. There aren't any rugs in the rooms."

He took the steps with care, his relaxed posture hiding his anxiety. Pausing, he commented, "No one's ever called me a coward before."

"I don't believe I did."

"You implied . . ."

"I said I didn't want to think you were a coward. I challenged you to prove that you aren't."

"I don't have to prove anything to you." He kept his voice level, wondering if she realized just how angry she'd made him.

"I agree, but you have a lot to prove to yourself."

He shook his head in consternation, acknowledging that he couldn't dismiss Bliss as shallow or self-serving. Her insights were right on target, but he nevertheless resented her attempt at manipulation.

Moreover, he didn't appreciate her comprehension, because he didn't want to think of her as an ally. He operated alone, personally and professionally. That was his style, and he intended to keep it that way. Theirs had to remain a casual relationship.

"You may be small, but you're tough."

She chuckled. "So I've been told. Ready?"

He nodded, amazement and grudging admiration surging through him as he contemplated the steel in Bliss Rowland's character. He couldn't recall ever meeting anyone quite like her. "Ready."

"The dining room is quite spacious. It's about thirty feet long and nearly as wide. Sideboards line three of the walls. The upper third of each wall is unobstructed glass, which floods the room with light during the day and makes it easy to see the stars on a clear night. There are also two sets of very tall French doors that lead out to the rose garden. The dining room is typical of most of the high-ceilinged formal rooms in the mansion."

Bliss placed his hand on the top edge of a high-backed upholstered chair as she spoke. "I generally take meals in the kitchen, but I thought today it might be nice to eat in here, since it's our first meal together. The table seats eighteen. There are eight chairs on either side of it and one at each end. We'll sit opposite one another."

Micah listened to her footsteps as she made her way around the table. Once she seated herself, he pulled out his chair and sat down but kept his hands in his lap. "You forgot something."

"Did I?"

"The chandelier above the table. Crystal, isn't it?"

"Tear-drop crystal. I've always loved the sound it makes when there's a breeze." She took her napkin and spread it across her lap. "I want you to feel comfortable here, Micah."

He knew the smile he produced looked strained. Oddly he feared making an ass of himself in front of her. Her opinion mattered a great deal to him, he realized, in spite of the decision he'd made to repay her for her previous cruelty. Mattered despite his decision of just minutes ago to relegate her to the status of a casual and meaningless acquaintance.

He exhaled a gust of pure frustration. Then his sense of smell alerted him to the food in front of him, and he discovered that his hunger momentarily eclipsed his anger.

Lifting his hands, Micah ran his fingertips along the edge of the table. He measured the width of his place setting and made certain of the location of his silverware and napkin while he grappled with the anxiety he felt.

"As you've discovered, your plate is directly in front of you. Since it's round, try thinking of it as a clock. Most people who share a meal with you in the future will wonder if they're supposed to tell how your food is situated on your plate. Many will feel reluctant to ask, though, so it's up to you to encourage them to do it. You'll alleviate their sense of helplessness and any inclination they might feel to cut your food for you, which invariably embarrasses everyone concerned. It also tells them that you aren't afraid of references to your lack of vision."

"The nurses insisted on feeding me. I hated it," Micah admitted as he ran the tips of his fingers around the edge of the plate to measure its size.

"I don't blame you. Forced dependence on others is the pits, especially when it's unnecessary. All right, then, let's get started," she encouraged him. "At twelve o'clock you'll find ham-and-cheese finger sandwiches. There are apple wedges and a cluster of green grapes at three o'clock, turkey finger sandwiches at six o'clock, and julienned carrots and celery, as well as cucumber slices, at nine o'clock."

Concentrating on his mental image of the place setting in front of him, Micah located the linen napkin positioned beside his plate, shook it loose, and placed it in his lap.

"There's a glass of orange juice four inches above the tip of your knife," Bliss explained. "Six inches farther to the right is a filled water glass. I've also placed a carafe of coffee in the center of the table, as well as two mugs, a platter of extra sandwiches, and a tray of brownies."

He inched his fingers toward the juice glass, grazed the base of it with the tip of one finger, and then wrapped his hand around it. Before he lifted the glass to his lips, Micah asked, "Are we alone?"

"Of course. I didn't think you'd appreciate an audience just yet. When you don't mind company other than me, we'll graduate to the kitchen. It's a less formal environment, and I prefer it. I think you will too." She paused, exhaled softly, then fell silent.

As he listened for her next comment, Micah drank half the contents of his juice glass before setting it back on the table. "What's wrong?" he asked, her silence starting to unsettle him. Her hesitation surprised him, because he knew by now that she tended to speak her mind.

"I understand how vulnerable you feel right now. Even though I'm not very subtle some of the time, I wouldn't ever do anything to compromise your dignity. If I have a criticism, I'll express it privately. All right?"

Micah nodded. He felt at a loss. He realized that she was trying to bridge the gap between them and under other circumstances might even have given her credit for understanding how unbalanced his world had become; but he still couldn't get completely past her remark about cowardice.

"I don't know about you, but I'm starving."

"You're good at this," he conceded, the manners ingrained in him during his youth emerging.

"Thank you."

He heard pleasure as well as surprise in her voice. "You were right before. I am angry." Micah carefully took one of the sandwiches from his plate as he spoke, but despite his hunger he simply held it. "I loathe what's happened."

"I know."

It took him a moment to realize that there was no pity in her voice. He felt a certain amount of relief, because pity was the last emotion he wanted to inspire in a woman. Even a woman who infuriated him one moment and then bewildered him with her compassion the next. "Perhaps you do," he said quietly, his voice reflective.

"What you're feeling is normal, but you can't let it cripple you."

"Are we eating the same meal?"

"Of course. Who do you think fixed it?" She laughed suddenly. "Mother never learned her way around the kitchen, but our cook taught me the fine art of finger sandwiches. Just be glad I didn't decide to feed you minced pimiento and cream cheese."

"Sounds awful."

"Doesn't it just?" she answered. "I could never stomach those sandwiches."

He could hear the lingering humor in her voice, and liked the sound more than he wanted to admit. Micah felt some of his tension ease, but he didn't relinquish all of his wariness.

Too hungry to delay eating any longer, he brought the sandwich to his lips and took a bite. He nearly groaned with relief when he tasted the slices of honey-glazed ham and Swiss cheese. He focused on filling his empty stomach, carefully treating his plate like the face of a clock as he selected his food. They ate in companionable silence, the sound of the surf and the fragrance of the island flowers enchancing the ambience of their first shared meal.

"You're an odd mix of patience and temper," Micah observed once he'd taken the edge off his hunger.

"I'm half Irish."

"That explains it."

"So I've been told," she replied. "You mentioned the Pacific Northwest as home. Is your family still there?"

"All except my baby sister."

For the first time in several weeks Micah thought of Leah, her husband, and their son, and the reason they no longer resided near the rest of the Holbrook family. He missed them, but their new identities and relocation to a small New England college town lessened his worry about their well-being. Micah knew they would survive the terrorist threat that had almost taken Leah's life, but his forced separation from them had taken its toll. Brett was not only his younger sister's husband, but his best friend and a former co-worker. He longed to contact them. He trusted them, and he knew they would provide understanding and moral support as he awaited the results of his experimental surgery.

"Do you come from a large family, Micah?"

He nodded and shifted his thoughts to his other loved ones. A smile flickered at the edges of his mouth. "Two brothers, three sisters, my parents, of course, and countless cousins, aunts, and uncles."

"How wonderful. I can hear the affection in your voice. You love them all very much, don't you?"

"Of course," he answered, his voice gruff. He rarely spoke of his family. For the sake of their safety he'd learned not to during his years in Naval Intelligence.

"You're fortunate to have them in your life.

Why don't you want them to know what's happened to you?"

He stiffened. "This doesn't concern them."

"How can it not?"

"My mother's a nurse, and she has her hands full with my father. He's got serious cardiac problems."

"And you don't want to become an unnecessary burden?"

"Precisely."

"Don't you think they can decide for themselves what's best for them?" she asked.

"I won't have my mother turning her home into a hospital ward, which is exactly what she'd feel compelled to do if . . . if the surgery fails." He hated even saying the words.

"What's plan B? What will you do if the surgery isn't successful?"

"You tell me," Micah shot back, his patience with this particular subject at an end.

"I shouldn't have to tell you."

"I'm not ready to think about it."

"You're not being very realistic, which surprises me. You know as well as I do that preparation is half the battle when you're dealing with adversity. Doesn't Cyrus call it an anticipatory battle plan? Perhaps you should start exploring some of your options for the future." When he failed to respond, she asked, "Doesn't your family deserve to know what you're up against so they can prepare themselves for the first time they see you? Or don't you intend to have anything to do with them if the surgery fails?"

Hearing her articulate some of the thoughts he'd had in recent weeks made him realize how ludicrous it would be to cut himself off from his loved ones, but he refused to acknowledge how close she'd come to the truth. "My family isn't up for discussion, so find another topic."

She did, but so smoothly that she startled him. "I realize that most of your work is classified, but I'd like to know more about the explosion in Central America."

He felt his appetite fade. He loathed thinking about that day, especially since he could recall only bits and pieces of the incident when he was awake. His nights were different, of course—haunted by a kaleidoscope of violent images that made it impossible for him to sleep restfully.

"Why?" Micah asked, his voice low and wary.

"Cyrus almost died."

"Why do you call him by his first name?"

"We have an odd relationship," she told him candidly. "Unless I'm speaking to him face-to-face or on the telephone he often seems like a stranger. So, are you going to tell me about the explosion?"

He frowned. "I can't."

"You don't want to talk about it?"

"I can't remember most of what happened," he admitted. "My memories are . . . fragmented."

"Do you have nightmares?"

Her voice held a gentleness that made Micah shift uncomfortably in his chair. He reached for his water glass, in his haste knocking it over. He swore viciously as he closed his extended hand into a tight fist and slammed it against the tabletop. Then he heard something else thud against the table and froze.

"For heaven's sake!" Bliss exclaimed with a laugh that sounded totally natural. "We're a pair, aren't we? No harm done, though. All we did was give the table a little water bath."

Still furious with himself, Micah remained silent. A few minutes later Bliss said, "There, the water's all mopped up. How about coffee and brownies now?"

Micah nodded slowly. Although still embarrassed by his clumsiness, he couldn't get beyond the fact that Bliss had deliberately spilled her own glass of water in order to make him feel better. A part of him fought her compassion, but a deeper and far more vulnerable part of him felt a profound gratitude.

He listened to her get up from her chair, make her way around to his side of the table, and remove his plate. "How old are you?" he asked as she poured coffee, took his right hand, and brought it to the side of the mug with an unconscious grace and thoughtfulness he reluctantly appreciated. Even though he realized that there was nothing even remotely sexual about her touch, he felt seduced by her nearness and her fragrance.

"The coffee's hot and black. There are two brownies on the plate in front of you. And I'm twenty-eight," she said, answering his question as she made her way back to her chair. "You're thirty-eight, aren't you?"

"How did you know?"

"Something Cyrus said, I suppose. What do you do for him these days, aside from dealing with the never-ending terrorist threat?"

These days? "This and that," he answered, perplexed by her choice of words.

"Another bad topic?"

"Not really."

"You're accustomed to being noncommittal about your career, aren't you?"

Micah shrugged. "For the most part." *These days?*

"Have you ever been married?"

"Of course not."

"Demands of the profession, I suppose."

Micah took a sip of coffee and then carefully returned the mug to the table. "I already told you—no permanent ties. It's easier all around."

"Sounds lonely. Don't you like brownies?" she asked.

He reached for his dessert fork. Using his left hand to hold the side of the plate, Micah tentatively cut a piece of brownie with the side of his fork and then speared it with the tines, but he hesitated as he pondered her previous observation. "It can be lonely, but you get used to it."

"I can't help wondering if people in government service should even bother to marry and have children," she said after sampling her own brownie and pronouncing it delicious. "They're hardly ever home."

"Do you resent Cyrus for being an absentee parent?"

"Not really. I just wish things had been different between us. My mother didn't remarry after they divorced."

"Do you blame him for putting the needs of his country before his family?"

"I did as a child."

"You're honest—I'll give you that."

"Would you prefer pretense? I'm not so public-spirited, and I definitely wasn't capable of nobility or forgiveness as a child. I wanted a father I could count on. He provided money for clothes and school and the gifts his secretaries purchased, but not much more. I'm the kind of person who requires time and communication when I care about someone. As far as I'm concerned, any other kind of a relationship is second best and a waste of time."

"What do you do when you aren't trying to rescue people from themselves?"

She laughed, and he sensed something oddly familiar about the sound. It gnawed at him because he couldn't place where he'd first heard it.

"I stay busy."

"Charity work?" he asked, an edge in his voice.

"I'm not an altruist by nature, although if I see something that needs to be done, I generally do it."

"At the risk of repeating myself, I have to say that you sound like Cyrus."

"I find that very hard to believe. He told me a long time ago that I reminded him of a butterfly, flitting from one thing to another when I'm bored or restless. I've actually got a fairly well-developed work ethic."

"He really said that to you?"

"Not verbatim, but that's what he meant."

"Perhaps you misread him."

"Perhaps."

"You don't think so, do you?"

Bliss sipped at her coffee before responding. "I honestly don't know what to think. Perhaps we'll have a chance to become better acquainted once he retires, but in the meantime I have a life to live, with as little regret as possible about the things I can't change or fix."

"Have we ever met before?" asked Micah, shifting gears without warning. She said nothing for several minutes. "Bliss?"

"Sorry. Yes, we've met before. It was about eleven years ago. I was attending school near London. Cyrus was in England on behalf of the White House."

"I don't remember."

"That doesn't surprise me. There's not much to remember."

Micah lapsed into silence as they finished their dessert and coffee. He also pondered her comment that there was nothing memorable about their first meeting, but the sound of her chair sliding back from the table and her footsteps as she circled around it distracted him from his thoughts.

Setting aside his napkin, Micah got to his feet. He felt Bliss slip a narrow length of smooth wood into his right hand. His instincts told him it was a cane, and he instantly rebelled against the idea of tapping his way through the mansion.

She anticipated his anger. "Before you hit

me with this thing, let me tell you about it. All right?"

"So talk."

"My grandfather was an avid bird-watcher. He loved taking long walks around the estate, but some of the terrain is quite rugged, especially around the bluffs on the north side of the property. During a particularly nasty tropical storm when I was a little girl, a fruitwood tree fell across one of his favorite paths. He said he took it as a sign that he didn't have to pretend to be as nimble as a mountain goat while he took his daily exercise, so he carved a half-dozen walking sticks from the trunk of the fruit tree, gave them to his closest friends, and kept one for himself. End of story."

"I don't need it," he insisted.

Bliss smoothed her fingertips over the back of his hand. Micah felt her gentleness, and he ached to draw her into his arms. Clutching the cane even more tightly, he tried to banish the erotic images that flashed, unbidden, through his mind.

"Grandfather was a good man—and also very proud and fiercely independent. Like you, Micah. But he wasn't a fool, and I know you aren't either. How about a compromise? Take his walking stick back to your room and think about the freedom it will give you. Try it on for size without an audience. The final decision is obviously yours. I'm just asking you to meet me halfway on this."

"You're asking a lot."

"I know," she whispered. "Believe me, I know."

Despite his conflicted emotions, he was pleased when Bliss looped her arm through his and guided him to the steps at the entrance to the dining room. She paused a fraction of a second before the first step. Reading her body language with an ease that surprised him, Micah automatically responded to her subtle cue. They climbed the two steps and walked across the foyer together.

"How about a walk on the beach this afternoon?" Bliss asked as they paused at the hallway entrance. "It's a perfect day outside, and you must be feeling cooped up by now."

Because he craved far more from her than a compassionate touch and guided tour of a beach he wouldn't be able to see, Micah stepped away from her. His senses warned him that he was near a wall. Extending his left hand, he slid his fingertips across an expanse of cool marble. "I've had enough torture for one day," he said dismissively.

"Micah?"

Determined not to become disoriented by her soft voice, he paused, but he didn't turn around.

"I enjoyed our brunch. Thank you for joining me. If you need me, one of the staff will help you locate me."

I need you now, he nearly shouted. *I need you naked and tucked beneath me. I need you to share your passion and your laughter while I bury myself in your body. I need you to help me forget what's happened to me, if only for a few hours.*

Micah walked away from her without a word, his spine rigid, his head held high, and the walking stick gripped in his right hand, although he refused to use it. He made his way down the long hallway and into his suite without incident. Closing the door behind him, he sank back against it and let the cane fall from his fingers, doubting that he would ever feel in control of his life again.

FIVE

Bliss needed to believe that Micah would find a way to get beyond his stiff-necked pride. She refused to cater to his moody behavior during their time together, which she deliberately limited to a few hours each day. She treated him like a sighted man, and she refrained from offering him anything more than guidance, friendship, and patience.

Despite her repeated urging, Micah refused to leave the mansion. He spent nearly all of his time in his suite, although he took meals with Bliss in the dining room. He reluctantly spoke to her, but only when she asked him a direct question. Frustrated by his long silences during their shared hours, she nevertheless continued her attempts to draw him out. By the fourth morning of his stay at Rowland House, Bliss despaired that she'd have to use dynamite to force him out of the mansion; but then he surprised her.

Bliss found Micah at the water's edge late that afternoon. She stood on the low bluff that overlooked the estate's private beach and paused to watch him. She noted the determined look on his face, and she viewed with pleasure the courage he exhibited as he made his way along the shoreline. He held her grandfather's walking stick, using it and the low waves that frothed and bubbled around his bare ankles to maintain his course.

She wanted to applaud his emergence from the cocoon of fear that had kept him indoors for the last four days, but she knew better than to make a big deal of his decision. She saw him pause in the low surf and lift his face to the sun. Warm Caribbean air gusted against his large body, ruffling his golden hair and molding his T-shirt and gym shorts to his muscular chest and narrow hips.

Bliss felt her senses sparkle with response to his masculinity. Simply looking at Micah, she realized, reinforced the attraction that simmered inside her. She nearly groaned, realizing the arousal he inspired in her was too pronounced to dismiss.

She finally summoned the effort required to move beyond her reaction to Micah as she abandoned the bluff and crossed the beach. With every step she took, Bliss reminded herself that helping him adjust had to be her first priority. She must ignore the emotional war taking place in her heart, not to mention the desire she felt every time she looked at him or thought about him.

"You've discovered my favorite stretch of beach," she announced so he would know he wasn't alone. "The sand is as fine-grained as sugar and almost as white."

Micah turned abruptly, misstepped, and then steadied himself with the walking stick.

"I didn't mean to startle you."

"You didn't," he insisted.

Bliss knew he was lying. She instantly regretted disturbing him, because she realized that the last thing he needed was to feel disoriented. Courage, she knew, could be fragile, especially in the early stages of rediscovering one's place in the world. She watched the muscles in his body ripple with tension, saw him lift his chin the way he always did when he felt threatened or defensive. Bliss moved to within a few feet of him, but she instantly quelled the urge to reach out to him even though her fingertips tingled.

"Have you been out here very long?"

"Long enough."

"I missed you at lunch. Weren't you hungry?"

He shrugged and turned his head. Gulls screeched overhead, and a cruise ship in the distance announced its impending arrival at the Charlotte Amalie Harbor with a succession of horn blasts.

"What's wrong, Micah?"

He stiffened, prompting Bliss to wonder if he felt uncertain about making his way back to the mansion on his own. She impulsively took his free hand and laced their fingers together. She needed to touch him, she realized, however impersonal or brief the contact. She savored the strength of his fingers and the warmth of his skin as he clasped her hand. Sensations she fought to ignore sizzled in her veins, but she managed to keep her voice even as she suggested, "Why don't we walk together?"

Instead of agreeing to her suggestion or stepping forward, Micah startled her by turning toward her. He adjusted his stance, tossed aside the walking stick, and seized her hips. Finding herself parked between his powerful thighs, Bliss flattened her hands against his chest.

"How much longer are you going to keep this up?" he taunted her.

Bewildered, she frowned. "I don't understand."

"Don't you?" he demanded.

Bliss paled. He obviously realized how much she wanted him. She felt embarrassed by his discovery of her attraction to him, as well as unnerved by the seductive feel of his hands curved over either side of her hips. "No, Micah, I don't understand," she insisted.

Even though she craved his touch, she continued to fear the temptation he presented. She also feared her inability to resist the desire and sensual curiosity coursing through her. She sensed that Micah would be extraordinary as a lover, but the risk of being used and then abandoned still terrified her. She tensed as she stood before him.

"Don't freeze up on me," he said, his voice so low that she strained to hear his words.

"Then don't behave this way."

"I've wanted to do this for days," he muttered as he gathered her into the golden heat of his body and lowered his head.

"Micah . . ." The sun disappeared. Alarm bells clanged in her head. Bliss felt disoriented, as though the world had tilted to an odd angle without any warning. She also felt every muscular inch of his imposing frame and every breath he took as he molded her against his body. "We . . ."

He grazed her lips with his own, stilling her protest as he brushed against her sensitive skin. She felt his tongue dart out to trace her lower lip. Stunned by his tender assault, she went very still.

"Micah," she whispered, but her voice contained disbelief, not warning.

He silenced her once more with amazing ease by shifting her hips forward to nestle against the strength pulsing in his loins. Bliss trembled, but she couldn't seem to move away from him—she didn't really want to move away from him. She felt his hands glide up to her waist and knew she should flee, but she didn't. He spanned her narrow waist with his fingertips, then trailed them up her back as he simultaneously traced the seam of her lips with the tip of his tongue. She sighed, her breath mingling with his as her resistance ebbed.

Clasping her head between his hands, Micah delved past her parted lips, his intrusion sending shock waves through her. Bliss moaned, the sound a feeble protest that turned into an unwitting invitation. Angling his mouth, Micah slanted his lips over hers and claimed the seductive heat that lay beyond. Skill and tenderness dominated his sensual foray, and Bliss knew she was on the verge of giving him anything he wanted.

"So sweet," he murmured against her lips.

Bliss felt her senses explode. Her wits scattered like debris strewn about by a violent wind, and she gave up the fight.

She sank into Micah's kiss, parting her lips and opening herself to his seductive exploration like a bud shyly embracing the glow of the sun. She welcomed every erotic stroke of his tongue as it dipped repeatedly into the depths of her mouth, just as she relished the possessive feel of his hands when he slid them down over her shoulders to her back so he could gather her even closer.

Bliss vaguely wondered if he could taste her hunger. She tasted his. She knew she would remember the hot, spicy flavor for as long as she lived, but then she tasted something more, something that hinted at darkness and danger when he deepened his search of her secrets.

Bliss sensed the change in him the instant it began, just as she felt it in the almost desperate way he plundered her mouth, his tongue thrusting and dipping ever more forcefully, his teeth nipping at her lips. She tensed when he gripped her shoulders. His fingers dugs into her, and he held her so tightly that she felt overpowered by his strength. When she heard him groan, she knew she had to stop him, and suddenly wrenched free.

Micah didn't attempt to stop her, but simply struggled for control. All she heard for several minutes was the mingled sound of their harsh breathing. Bliss finally opened her eyes and risked a glance at his face. In the tension etched into his features, she glimpsed his full awareness of what had just happened, as well as his regret that she'd pulled away from him.

"We can't . . ."

"You're wrong," he insisted, anger and frustration expressed in his sharp tone of voice. "We can. I need you."

She shuddered, not with desire but with sadness. "You don't need *me*. You need any woman who'll have you right now, because all you want to do is forget for a little while. Please . . ." Her voice cracked, and she fell silent.

Grappling with her emotions and fighting tears, Bliss turned to stare out across the aquamarine waves that swelled and dipped all the way to the horizon. She shivered despite the sultry air buffeting her body and the currents of heat still surging through her bloodstream.

"Please what?" he demanded.

"Please don't do this to me. Even though I care about you, it's a bad idea." Bliss bent down, retrieved the walking stick, and placed it in his right hand. "I need to get back to the house."

"Why is it a bad idea?"

"It just is."

He swore, the word coarse enough to make her flinch, then extended the walking stick in front of him with practiced ease and started up the beach.

"Wait, Micah." She followed after him, relieved when he finally paused on the bluff. Grateful that the security personnel patrolling the estate continued to keep their distance, Bliss felt compelled to be honest with him. "Making love means a commitment to me. I can't be casual about it."

He exhaled and shoved his fingers through an unruly lock of hair that had fallen across his forehead. "I don't feel casual, Bliss. I've never felt less casual in my life."

She moved closer, then hesitated because she knew that all she really wanted to do was walk back into his arms. "I thought I might take a drive. Would you like to come with me? It might help us both relax." Even she heard how feeble her suggestion sounded.

"Forget it."

"Then I'll walk back to the house with you," she offered, worry in her eyes as she studied him.

He shrugged, but the arousal of his body and the tension tightening his muscles made the deliberately nonchalant gesture appear pretentious. "Suit yourself."

Shoulders squared, body aching with need,

and spine rigid, Micah silently navigated the stretch of beach from the mansion. Although acutely aware of Bliss's presence at his side, he forced himself beyond the erotic images playing through his mind and concentrated on each step he took. He throbbed with need, and his blood simmered, but his pride was alive and well. He didn't intend to humiliate himself by tripping and falling at her feet.

As he walked, Micah couldn't erase his memory of the feel of Bliss in his arms or the answering burst of passion in her response to him, but neither could he ignore his conscience. She thought he wanted nothing but a quick tumble. She was wrong: In his heart of hearts Micah wanted far more from her than sex, although he felt reluctant to admit that she'd aroused his deepest emotions as well as his body. She'd brought to life longings from the past that would put an end to the isolation necessitated by his profession, longings he'd set aside as foolish and irresponsible many years before.

Bliss Rowland fascinated him with her strength of purpose, and she tantalized him with her gentleness and compassion. She also made him achingly aware of her deeply sensual nature. He wanted more of that secret self she rarely revealed. Much more.

She perplexed him, too, because he couldn't

get a fix on her emotions, which seemed aloof at times and intensely complex at others. He'd deliberately kept his distance from her in recent days, not only because he felt so uneasy about the prospect of facing life as a blind man, but also in an effort to hold his physical desire and emotional hunger at bay. The thought of becoming dependent on Bliss—or anyone—unnerved him.

He wished they had met under different circumstances—a love affair at this point in his life would be disastrous. Neither did he want to use her because he knew that Bliss Rowland was the kind of woman who deserved devotion and sensitivity, qualities he had in short supply right now.

Micah exhaled harshly, the hunger in him expanding instead of retreating as he neared the mansion's patio. Her taste lingered on his lips, just as the heat of her skin and ripeness of her hourglass-shaped figure still dominated his sensory memory.

Micah almost resented her for the desire she unknowingly inspired, even though it made him feel more alive than he'd felt in years. Suddenly too frustrated to maintain such rigid control over himself, he purposely veered into her path. He felt her loss of balance when her hand brushed against his hip. Grabbing her, he took the final steps to the sheltered patio with Bliss tucked against his side.

"Talk about not paying attention. I'm sorry, Mi—"

He cut her off, his instincts those of a vital male—a sighted male—as he brought her against his body and claimed her parted lips. He needed her, and that was all the justification he could think of for his impulsive behavior as he drank in the startled sound she made, savored the feel of her hands as she gripped his waist in order to get her balance, and said a silent prayer that she wouldn't feel the need to jerk free of him again.

He staked his claim, without desperation this time and with the intent of sending a clear message. He wanted her.

Micah knew he lacked his customary finesse as he sipped at her with the possessiveness of a longtime lover who knew his mission, but he didn't care. He trusted his instincts—the way Bliss had forced him to—as he tenderly assaulted her senses and tasted her essence. The sweetness of her burst across his interior landscape like a series of perfectly timed detonations.

He felt her hands slide around his waist, then the pressure of her slender fingers as she held on to him. Micah felt overwhelmed, combustible, on the verge of being incinerated by the fever raging in his mind and body. He struggled to tame his response to Bliss, because he feared frightening her into another withdrawal. He lifted his head and filled his lungs with breath. His hands shook as he smoothed them up and down Bliss's arms, and he prayed that she wouldn't walk away from him.

"Touching you is like touching fire," he whispered when he found his voice and the strength to speak.

Pressing his lips to her temple, he inhaled the seductive scent of her skin and hair before he trailed his hands down her narrow back. He felt the tremor that moved through her like a slow, sensual serenade on a warm summer night. The press of her thighs, the cradle of her femininity, the soft swell of her stomach, and her high, full breasts made a heated imprint against his body. He shuddered, need and a thousand other emotions splintering his heart.

Paying close attention to her with all of his senses, Micah shifted his hands forward and skimmed his fingertips over her uptilted breasts. He nearly groaned at the perfection beneath his hands. "No bra," he muttered.

"No bra," she echoed in a stunned little voice.

He cupped her breasts, measuring their weight with gentle hands. "Why not?"

She sighed, the sound ragged and very sexy.

"I hate feeling confined. I'm not that big, anyway."

He covered her with his hands. He felt her nipples harden and stab into his palms. Desire spiked to new heights within his body, and regret suffused him that they were both still clothed and not stretched out atop a comfortable bed.

"You're just right," he said. "I want to put my mouth on you. I want to taste every inch of you, and then I want to do it again."

Bliss shivered, but she didn't speak.

"You want me."

"I can't let myself want you."

"But you do."

She shook her head, then moaned softly when his hands tightened over her firm breasts. "This is crazy," she gasped. "We can't indulge in this kind of behavior."

Micah decided to prove her wrong. He gently flicked his thumbnails over her nipples, her light cotton shirt a meaningless barrier even though it sheathed her from prying eyes. Her body responded in a heartbeat. Micah saw no reason to restate the obvious. He simply waited.

"You aren't being fair to either one of us."

"Life's not fair. Besides, you want me. I can feel how much you want me."

"I'm more than body parts. I'm a person with feelings."

"I don't want to be fair, Bliss." He lowered his head and sampled the taste of her lips once more. When he paused, he drew her close and held her with a tenderness that felt vaguely foreign to him. "Don't ask me to be fair. I don't know how right now."

She went very still. Micah got the impression she'd all but stopped breathing. "Tell me what you're thinking," he urged.

"Are you finished?" she asked.

Her voice, so deathly calm, sounded as though it belonged to a stranger. Baffled, he brought his hands up to her face and skimmed her features with his fingertips, but she might as well have been cast in stone for all the expression he found.

Bliss jerked free of him without warning and tugged her shirt into place. "Stop this, Micah. I refuse to be treated like a slut."

Her temper and her words shocked him. He knew she could be stubborn, but he felt ill prepared to deal with the genuine anger he heard in her voice. His own temper sparked to life. "I guess your pity for the blind man doesn't extend to his bedroom."

"Damn you. I don't pity you, and I never will."

"Right," he muttered scathingly.

His desire dwindled, but it didn't burn out. He wanted her too badly, and he knew his attire did nothing to conceal his aroused body. For the moment he didn't care. Micah wanted her to see her effect on him, even if he couldn't see her swollen breasts. The nipples had to be the palest coral, he decided as he stood there, his expression dangerous and his fists clenched at his sides.

"I don't like one-night stands, and that's all you're offering me. I'm worth more, Micah Holbrook. Much more."

"You wanted me." When she didn't respond, he reminded her, "I tasted you, Bliss. I tasted your hunger, and I felt your heat. You're on fire for me, and you know it. What just happened between us was not one-sided," he declared belligerently.

"Yes, I want you, but I'm not a part of your vacation package, so get that notion out of your head."

Shocked by her unexpected crudeness, he frowned.

"Don't look so blasted surprised," she chastised him. "I'm not so stupid as to deny that you're capable of arousing me physically. Of course I want you—I'd have to be dead and buried not to—but there's something I definitely do not want, and that's your state of mind. It's negative, so kindly keep it and your hands to yourself."

"Then change it," he challenged. "Change my negative attitude, since it bothers you so much."

"That's your job, not mine," she shot back. "All I can do is give you the tools. The rest is up to you."

He knew she was right, even though it irked him to admit it. He heard her footsteps as she crossed the patio. "Bliss, I'm . . ." The words he wanted to say were stuck in his throat by the time she paused on the threshold of her suite. "Oh, hell, just forget it."

"You were wrong before, Micah," she told him, her voice solemn. "I can't rescue you or anyone else. So save yourself, because you'll have to live with the consequences if you don't."

As he stood there listening to her footsteps fade, he sensed a wealth of unexpressed emotion in her words, but only after he worked beyond her implication that he was wallowing in self-pity. What had begun as a forced trip to Saint Thomas had graduated to a battle royale between two strong-willed people.

Micah felt as if he'd gone to war without any weapons, although his gut instinct insisted that he'd struck a nerve with Bliss. Beneath her determination he'd discovered tremendous vulnerability and a tumultuous undercurrent of passion—passion she obviously felt compelled to control. Her control had slipped, though, revealing a side of herself that both amazed and seduced him.

He realized that he'd finally honored his vow to repay her for making him feel so vulnerable, but instead of experiencing triumph or satisfaction, he felt like a jerk for pushing her so hard.

As he made his way into his suite, Micah promised himself that he would prove to Bliss he was worth trusting as a lover. For the first time since the explosion in Central America, he felt committed to embracing the challenges posed by his lack of vision. His blindness hadn't prevented Bliss from being attracted to him, and he wasn't going to let it prevent him from making her his.

In the tension-filled days that followed, Bliss felt as though someone were dangling her from an emotional precipice. She constantly struggled to control her deepening feelings for Micah, but even she came to recognize the futility of the endeavor. She didn't mention their passionate encounter and neither did he, but it remained a constant in her consciousness. Although she refused to hide from him, she carefully guarded her emotions during their hours together.

Despite his impatience and frustration with his situation, she sensed a subtle change in his attitude, and she employed it as she encouraged him to convert the senses he'd carefully honed in his work with Naval Intelligence to meet his current needs. Even though he remained reserved and kept his distance from her whenever possible, he cooperated with her efforts to help him regain his independence.

She taught him a color-coding system for his clothing, and saw an immediate rise in his confidence. When he admitted that he'd been an avid reader, she provided him with books on tape. She also insisted that he accompany her to a board meeting of the island's school for the blind. Although he said little about it, Bliss knew the experience had made a profound impression on him, especially when she introduced him to several young students who were members of the school's track team.

She initiated a policy of reading aloud to him the parts of the newspaper Micah particularly enjoyed. She also gave him a beginner's primer for the Braille alphabet and provided emotional support as he came to grips with the shocking reminder that he might never regain his vision.

Bliss insisted that Micah become acquainted with the various paths that covered the grounds of the sprawling estate, as well as the three-mile-long stretch of beachfront. She reminded him that he needed exercise, and her reward arrived a week later when she spotted him jogging the length of the beach after carefully inspecting the area with the walking stick. Even the security personnel guarding the estate noticed Micah's progress and commented on it when they spoke to Bliss.

She spent time in her studio each afternoon, her sculpting an outlet to express her feelings for Micah. When they were together, she encouraged, cajoled, and refused to take no for an answer. When she was alone, she prayed for the strength not to lose control of her emotions. Despite her valiant efforts, she fell deeply and helplessly in love with the courageous, and very complex Micah Holbrook.

Dr. Chalmers visited every other morning, but he confined his medical observations to the reports he phoned to Micah's doctors in Washington. For his part Micah volunteered nothing about the examinations to Bliss.

Emotionally stretched to the limit following the often tense hours she spent with Micah, Bliss returned to her suite each night exhausted but too sexually aroused to sleep well. She paced her bedroom far into the night. When she finally slept, her dreams were filled with images so erotic that she frequently wakened trembling, drenched in perspiration, and acutely aware that Micah restlessly paced the patio just beyond the closed French doors of her room. She longed to go to him, but exerted all the force of her will to refrain from doing so.

By Micah's tenth day at the estate, Bliss reverted to monitoring his progress as he perfected the skills she'd shared with him. Although he never acknowledged her efforts and she never questioned his motivation—which she privately assumed was a combination of pride and anger—she felt gratified by his new attitude, as well as the concentration and commitment he brought to relearning tasks he'd once taken for granted.

That same day Bliss consciously stopped pretending that she wasn't in love with Micah. She was, and she knew she needed to acknowledge and deal with her feelings, because they weren't going to disappear anytime soon.

SIX

It was well after midnight a few evenings later when Bliss settled into the wicker swing on the patio she shared with Micah. She savored her privacy now that everyone except the security guards patrolling the perimeter of the estate had retired for the night.

Closing her eyes, Bliss concentrated on clearing away the emotional debris that littered the landscape of her mind. She needed to relax.

She rocked back and forth, and the gentle swaying motion of the swing eventually lessened some of the tension that had driven her from her bed. Bliss took pleasure in the silence of the calm night and the balmy breeze that flowed across her nightgown-clad body, although the scented air served to sensitize her skin even more than usual.

After a while she brought her slender legs up and wrapped her arms around them. Resting her chin on her upraised knees, she stared at the star-studded sky. She'd already accepted that her desire for Micah would remain a constant within her well beyond his departure. He still symbolized all the fantasies she'd had about love and being loved by the right man, fantasies she'd nurtured since their first, long-ago encounter.

She sighed, the melancholy sound blending with the breeze whispering around her. Unable to stop herself, Bliss shifted her gaze to the closed French doors that led into Micah's suite.

She pondered her efforts to dismiss him from her thoughts in recent days. Because she loved him, she invariably failed. She felt as though he occupied every corner of her world. Each night she spent alone in her bed felt like an endurance test. She began each day in a state of emotional fatigue, knowing that only Micah, a man she knew she couldn't claim for herself, could ever satisfy her soul-deep hunger for love.

Even though she sought refuge in the privacy of her studio every afternoon, he remained the focus of her attention. If anything, he dominated her thoughts even more.

The artist in her had finally seized control, forcing her to vent her complex emotions. She employed her talent in sculpting a bust of Micah that quickly came to life beneath her nimble fingers. Although it was nearly complete, Bliss couldn't bring herself to put the finishing touches on the work. She didn't want the process to end, any more than she wanted Micah to leave the estate.

Instead, she behaved like a woman possessed as she devoted herself to refining the sculpture. She made love to Micah each time she lost herself in the clay, abandoning in the process the restraint she manifested whenever they were together.

She allowed her emotions and her passion for him to rule her creative universe, and the end result possessed a vitality even she had failed to anticipate. Micah seemed to live and breathe beneath her fingertips, his rugged masculinity and courage as he confronted and overcome his fear of being permanently sightless reflected in the sculpture she'd created.

Bliss realized that she'd also captured his power over her. It had finally occurred to her that Micah Holbrook wasn't simply her ultimate fantasy; he was her ultimate terror, her very own heartbreaker, even if he didn't know it. He possessed the ability to shatter her dreams.

Bliss froze when the doors to Micah's suite suddenly opened. He stepped out onto the patio, his newly reclaimed self-confidence evident in his unhesitating stride and his posture as he approached her. She felt her pulse speed up as he drew nearer.

She shivered, then held her breath when he paused in front of her. Unable to stop herself, she let her gaze sweep across the moon-washed glory of his broad shoulders and muscular upper torso. The golden pelt that covered his chest, then narrowed to disappear beneath the waistband of the black silk pajama bottoms he wore, made her fingers tingle. His belly, which reminded her of a slab of stone, invited more than a visual inspection, as did his narrow hips and powerful legs.

She clenched her hands into tight fists. Her craving to touch him, to sink her fingers into that dense chest hair and then explore at her leisure the warmth and vitality of his entire body, nearly overwhelmed her. Sucking in enough air to fill her burning lungs, she dragged her greedy gaze up to the hard lines of his face.

Micah angled his head slightly. Bliss sensed he was trying to read her mood, and a part of her rejoiced at his willingness to use his intuition to his best advantage. Even though she knew she should speak to him, she didn't. Her heart felt wedged in her throat. She feared revealing her hunger for Micah, just as she feared making a fool of herself over him. For the first time since his arrival she realized that she didn't have the strength to put his needs before her own.

"Am I disturbing you, Bliss?"

"No," she whispered. When he didn't say anything else, she sensed that he was waiting for an invitation. "Join me if you'd like. It's very peaceful out here tonight." As he sat down beside her, she hoped her voice hadn't betrayed her inner tension, but she suspected it had.

Micah reached out, but Bliss caught his hand before he encountered her naked thigh and discovered that she wore nothing more than a gauzy silk nightgown.

"What's wrong?" he asked as he casually wove their fingers together.

His touch sent a faint tremor of response through her body. "Nothing."

"You don't usually deny the obvious."

"I'm not denying anything," she insisted, thinking how stupid she'd sound if she admitted that he was the reason she couldn't sleep.

"It's late. I'm usually the one who's restless at this hour of the night."

"I'm not restless."

"Then why aren't you in bed?"

"It was . . . too warm in my room."

"Try again," he suggested, patience resonating in his low voice.

"All right," she conceded. "I'm restless."

"Some people think I'm a good listener when they need to talk."

"It's personal. I'll work it out, but thank you for offering to help." Although startled by the ease with which he slipped his arm around her shoulders, she welcomed what she knew he considered casual contact and didn't try to shift away from him.

"It's no wonder you don't want to talk to me. I've been more than a little self-involved lately, haven't I?"

She smiled and indulged in the luxury of resting her head against his shoulder. "It goes with the territory, but you're forgiven. You've had a lot to deal with."

"I'm still *dealing*," he admitted. "And I'll have a lot more to learn if the surgery fails."

Pleased that he could now admit aloud the reality he faced, she nearly succumbed to the urge to applaud the strides he'd made in the last few weeks. "It's a daily process, Micah, but you'll make it over all the hurdles as long as you give yourself the time you need."

"You've been very generous with your patience. Most people would long ago have given up on me and sent me packing."

She didn't like the direction of his comments. "Let's save the testimonials for another time. I did what I wanted to do. Nothing more, and nothing less." *Liar*, her conscience taunted. *You haven't done one tenth of what you want to do with this man.*

"Your faith in people amazes me some of the time."

"Why? I've always believed in the strength of the human spirit. I guess it's kind of a religion with me. In your case it wasn't so much my having faith as it was my reminding you to look inward and trust yourself."

"You make it sound so simple, but we both know it wasn't and still isn't."

"At the risk of repeating a time-worn cliché, nothing worth achieving is simple," Bliss remarked. "You just needed the right tools and a friend with the personality of a drill sergeant."

He laughed at that, and savoring the low, rumbling sound, she realized how easily she could get used to having Micah in her life.

"You're not like any drill sergeant I've ever met."

"That'll be our secret," she suggested, humor edging into her voice before she could stop it.

"This is the first time you've really let your guard down with me. Why?"

Torn between blurting out the truth and indulging in a subterfuge that might protect her, she glanced up at him. After a long moment she exhaled softly and asked, "Honestly?"

He nodded. "Honestly."

"I'm attracted to you." She saw him flinch as though she'd struck him, but she forged ahead anyway. "I knew I couldn't risk letting my feelings get in the way of what you needed to accomplish during your stay at Rowland House. It would have softened my attitude and clouded my judgment, and I wouldn't have pushed you as hard as you needed to be pushed, especially at the beginning. I also didn't want to get involved in a casual affair. You have a life to go back to, and I've already told you how I feel about being used as a sexual safety net. That kind of relationship is too painful when it's over."

"Are you always this honest?" he asked quietly.

She sighed, aware that her candor often made people, especially sophisticated men, think she was terribly naive. "Yes, although not everyone appreciates it."

"I'd forgotten that there were women like you in the world."

"Oh?" *Fools?* she almost asked, but she managed not to make a complete idiot of herself.

"That's why there hasn't been a woman in my life for a long time."

"Oh."

"I'm starting to hear an echo."

She poked him in the ribs, then had trouble bringing her hand back to her lap, where she knew it belonged. Just the thought of exploring his body with her fingertips, and then following the same path with a string of hot, open-mouthed kisses, seduced both her imagination and her senses. "Be nice," she chided.

"Talk to me about London."

"Why?"

"I want to remember you."

"I've already told you there isn't much to remember."

"Don't hedge. You don't have to protect yourself or hide from me." Micah tucked her even closer, his arm snugging her against him so that she felt forged to him. "There was a time when I first got here that I would have used any weapon you provided as a means of hurting you, but I don't feel that way any longer."

Bliss understood his meaning. She'd provoked him during their earlier days together in order to penetrate his self-pity. At the time she'd suspected he would enjoy exacting a large penance from her, but she believed him now when he said he no longer felt that way.

"You were very kind to me in London."

"Don't kid yourself, Bliss. We both know

I'm not a kind man. I've made it this far by being a manipulative, bullheaded son of a—"

"You saved my life," she said in a rush. "One minute I was standing in a dress shop a few blocks from Harrods, and the next I was buried under rubble. I thought you were a living, breathing miracle when you pulled me out of that place."

He muttered a harsh word. "The IRA terrorist bombing."

"I didn't think there was any point in bringing it up. It's just as well you didn't remember me."

"Why?"

"You're actually going to make me say it, aren't you?"

"I don't understand."

He obviously didn't, she realized. "I had the most excruciating crush on you, and I know I wasn't at all subtle. I didn't want to remind you of my previous immature behavior during your current stay."

"You were a big-eyed little girl who refused to speak to me. Getting you to talk was like pulling teeth."

She smiled ironically. "I was a mouse, and I was scared witless. Nothing like that had ever happened to me before. I knew by your uniform that you were an American, so I felt safe with you."

"I rode to the hospital with you," he recalled aloud. "At first I thought you were in shock, because you wouldn't stop staring at me."

"I was in shock, but I was also afraid you'd disappear if I closed my eyes, and then I'd be back in that dress shop again. I wouldn't let go of your hand, so you stayed with me while the doctor stitched up my leg. You didn't leave the hospital until someone told you my father had been reached and someone would be arriving soon to be with me. I don't think you knew then that Cyrus is my father."

"A lot of water's gone under the bridge since," he said reflectively.

Bliss's smile dimmed altogether as she considered how little she'd progressed despite the passage of so many years. She loved Micah more than ever now, and she couldn't help wondering if that meant she'd gone backward instead of forward. Arrested emotional development, she concluded. "A lot can happen in eleven years."

"You've outgrown your shyness."

She shifted uncomfortably. "Not really. I'm at my best when I'm working in my studio."

"I should have remembered you."

"I wasn't important. No more than a blip on the screen of what I gather has been a very exciting life in Naval Intelligence."

He shifted their bodies so that they wound up knee-to-knee. Bringing his hands to her face, he cupped her cheek and traced the width of her full lower lip with his thumb. She held her breath, more unsure of herself than ever thanks to the tenderness of his touch.

"You've become very important to me, Bliss Rowland. I may not have seen your value when you were seventeen and frightened, but now I know your value as a woman and as an ally. Which means more to you? The past or the present?"

She studied him with the aid of the bright moonlight that splashed across his features. Although his eyes were still concealed by bandages, the angular lines of his face revealed his sincerity. Still, he posed a very real emotional threat to her.

"I'm only a temporary part of your life, Micah," she cautioned, her protective instincts lining up around her heart like a contingent of security guards. "Just as your stay at Rowland House is temporary. You'll get on with your life once you leave here. I know you'll remember me this time, but I'll just be a memory. That's all."

"You're wrong."

"No, I'm not—"

He placed a fingertip against her lips. "I

don't want to argue with you. Tell me about your life."

She resisted the urge to press her lips against the tip of his finger. When he lowered his hands to her shoulders, she commented, "You already know the high points. Lots of travel when I was young, good schools, interesting people, divorced parents." Bliss shrugged. "My work gets most of my attention."

"You mentioned a studio? Are you a painter?"

"A sculptor." Oddly enough, she felt almost reassured that he hadn't connected her to the public personna she periodically displayed to art critics around the world. She liked being known as Bliss Rowland, person, rather than Elizabeth Rowland, a sculptor of some renown.

She finally noticed Micah's silence, but it was the troubled expression on his face that made her ask, "Is something wrong?"

"It's your whole world, isn't it?"

Bliss stiffened beneath his hands. She hadn't expected this insight, and it heightened her anxiety. "Yes, it is."

He frowned. "You sound defensive."

"It's what I do, and I certainly don't have to justify it."

"Does it makes you happy?" he asked.

Although baffled by his motive for asking

such a question, she readily answered him. "Of course. I can't imagine doing anything else."

"Are you hiding behind your sculpting, the same way I've hidden behind my career?"

"I'm not hiding," she protested. "Micah, you're not making sense."

"It's a good way to avoid emotional commitment, especially if you do it to the exclusion of everything else."

"Is that what you've done?" she asked, determined to turn the tables on him because he was getting much too close to the truth.

"Is Cyrus the reason you wouldn't let me make love to you?" he demanded.

She stared at him, disconcerted by his question. She felt his fingers dig into her shoulders, but she didn't have the strength to protest his harsh grip.

"Is he, Bliss?" Micah asked sharply.

"He doesn't have a vote," she said, anger flaring inside her. "Change the subject, Micah."

"We're both loners, aren't we?"

She tried to shift backward, but he refused to free her. She sighed in exasperation. "Perhaps. What's your point?"

"I tried to get you into my bed for the wrong reasons. I shouldn't have tried to use you."

Surprised by his remark, she said, "I understood what you were doing."

"You don't understand now, though, do you? I still want you. Even more now than I did before. That hasn't changed. It won't change."

She felt her heart stop beating for a couple seconds. Loving him put her at a distinct disadvantage, and she suddenly resented him for it. "You can't possibly know for certain what you want or need. Your life is in a state of flux. So are your emotions."

"Why did you agree to help me?" he asked.

"We're going over old ground."

"Why, Bliss? Was it some misguided sense of obligation because of what happened in London?"

"Of course not. I'm not operating a charity here. I have a life, not to mention a demanding and rewarding career."

"Then why did you take time from your busy life for me and my problems?"

"Because . . ." She hesitated, unwilling to make an admission that would put her at his mercy. ". . . my father is your friend."

"Was it pity?"

"No!" she exclaimed, her green eyes sparkling like gemstones.

"Prove it!" He jerked her forward without warning.

Planting her open palms on his chest, Bliss

stiffened her arms and caught herself before she crashed into him. He kept his hands on her shoulders, eliminating the possibility of flight.

"I don't have to prove anything to you."

"Bliss, tell me the truth."

"You're behaving like a jerk," she accused, her fury with him surfacing completely.

"Guilty as charged."

She forced herself to try a calmer approach, even though her heart seemed to be racing at breakneck pace. "You're an attractive man, Micah. You can have any woman you want, but I'm not on the menu, so don't pick me."

"I'm selective. Very selective."

"Congratulations!" she snapped.

"Tell me you don't want me. Tell me you aren't attracted to me any longer."

She couldn't, so she didn't. She glared at him instead, forgetting for a moment that he couldn't see her facial expression. Making a last-ditch effort at the truth, Bliss humbled herself by quietly admitting, "You have the power to hurt me, Micah. I wouldn't survive an affair with you."

He groaned, brushed her hands aside, and brought her against his muscular chest. Wrapping his arms around her, he molded her against him in such a way that she felt the force of his heartbeat against her breasts. "I wouldn't hurt you for anything in the world. Don't you know that yet?"

Dazed by the currents of sensations spiraling through her body, Bliss wondered if she knew anything anymore. She felt naked, despite the silk that separated their upper bodies, and her breasts ached. She felt emotionally flayed. She'd never been more shaken by her desire for a man.

"Tell me how I'm supposed to survive the need I feel every time you're within ten feet of me," he demanded. "Convince me that I'm not your charity case of the month."

She struggled, twisting and turning in his arms, but to no avail. "I won't be treated this way, not by you or anyone else."

"Then let me treat you the way you deserve to be treated," he coaxed.

Micah claimed her lips, his assault on her senses tender yet insistent. Stunned by his passion, she trembled in his embrace as she sampled a foretaste of his leashed hunger. Bliss knew that no man had ever wanted her with such intense desire, or made her feel so on the verge of spinning completely out of control.

Her entire body pulsed and throbbed with the need to reach fruition in his arms. Even though she longed to surrender to him, she instinctively struggled against the consuming weakness that flowed through her, beckoning her, seducing her until she couldn't think clearly.

As Bliss circled his shoulders with her arms, she sensed the inevitability of their situation. Micah, she realized, whether by design or destiny, was on the verge of becoming the architect of her emotional downfall. Even as she silently cursed his power over her, she craved him as a lover.

"Tell me, Bliss," he urged in a low voice so filled with erotic tension that she wanted to burrow beneath his skin and stay there forever. "Tell me how I'm supposed to walk away from you."

His innate sensuality and her own fragile emotions conspired against her. She reached up and grazed his cheek with her fingertips in a gentle caress. She sighed, then moaned as he lowered his head and found her lips again.

"Micah . . ." she whispered shakily.

He trailed his fingers over her silk-covered nipples. She shuddered, falling silent as she arched into his touch. He muttered an indistinct phrase before he kissed her once more. Bliss savored his taste as she would have the finest vintage wine. His tongue delved deeply into her mouth as he pushed aside the thin straps of her nightgown.

Bliss felt the scarlet confection slide down her body and catch at her waist. Micah cupped her swollen breasts with such gentleness that she gasped. She held her breath until her lungs burned in protest. She willingly deepened their kiss, tangling her tongue with his in a sensual duel as he fondled her sensitive flesh.

Feeling feverish with needs too long denied and emotions too raw and too intense to contain or curtail, she clutched at Micah's shoulders, the tempered strength of his body finally hers to experience, the heat of his skin hers to explore and then taste at her leisure, and the glorious feel of his hands curved possessively over her breasts devastating what remained of her flagging resistance.

Awash in a tumult of sensation, Bliss whimpered softly. Micah took the sound into his mouth as he hugged her against his chest. She felt the tremors of need that ravaged his large frame and made his hands shake.

"Why me?" she asked when she could speak a few minutes later.

"Because I care about you, and I need you, and I think I'm fall—"

Panic flared inside her. "No, don't say anything else." She didn't want to hear him make a commitment he might regret later. She preferred the simplicity of honest need, shared need, and she half-convinced herself that such candor now would make their eventual parting easier for her.

Micah clasped her head between his hands, his long fingers tunneling into the thick black curls that capped her head and framed her face. "I'd give anything to be able to see you. I need to know what you're thinking and how you're feeling, and I'm certain your eyes would tell me if I could just look at you for a moment."

"This isn't about being able to see, Micah."

"I almost believe you."

"If you trust me, and I think you do, then you can believe me."

He freed her and got to his feet, but he didn't urge her to stand. He simply waited, one hand extended.

Bliss knew she could walk away. She realized that Micah's sense of personal honor demanded that he give her the option, but she knew it was useless to question the wisdom of her actions. Right or wrong, and despite the anguish she expected to suffer once he left Rowland House, she intended to make love to Micah.

Although nervous, Bliss found the courage to stand. Her nightgown slid past her hips and down her legs to pool at her feet. She slipped her hand into Micah's, the strength of his grip as his fingers closed tightly over hers all the reassurance she needed at the moment.

"My bedroom?"

"Yes," she whispered.

Once they stood beside the bed in his dark bedroom, Micah drew her into his arms and held her. She felt him shudder when he came into contact with her bare skin.

"Tell me what you want from me, Bliss."

She circled his narrow waist with her arms, pressed her cheek to his chest, and listened to his hammering heart. The final barrier tumbled away, leaving her more emotionally exposed than she'd ever been in her life. "I just want you."

Leaning down, he trailed his lips along the fragrant curve that joined her neck and shoulder. Bliss felt a flare of desire burst inside her. A second detonation came on the heels of the first one, and then a third one rocked her. She trembled, her fingers pressing into the muscled flesh at the base of his spine as she stood in the circle of his arms. Stripped of all emotional barriers, she knew in that moment that nothing would ever be the same between them again.

SEVEN

Micah wanted to take her slowly.

He wanted to handle her with finesse.

He wanted to be gentle and more thoughtful than he'd ever been with a woman in his entire life, but he knew in those first few seconds of holding Bliss in his arms that his need was too great.

He felt almost clumsy as he covered her breasts with his hands, even though she moaned at his encompassing touch. The richly seductive sound fueled his desire for her, and he sensed within himself a level of sensual volatility that threatened his control as a lover.

His sex surged against her softly curved belly, as if to mock him and all the illusions he'd ever had about control. He kneaded her satiny breasts. Her puckering nipples nudged delicately against the centers of his palms. Micah shuddered, but he clamped down on his desire, determined to be restrained, to be what she needed him to be.

He intended to arouse her until she was on the verge of coming apart in his arms, if only to prove to her that he deserved her passion and trust. She sabotaged his efforts almost instantly.

Pressing feverish kisses to his chest and throat, Bliss slowly trailed her fingertips over his narrow hips and then brought her hands forward. He tensed as she stroked his muscular, hair-rough thighs with a touch that was erotic and fingernails that tantalized. Micah muttered her name, his voice huskily sensual, his body seething with sensations too diverse to name.

Bliss paused and lifted her face. He felt and heard the shaky gust of air that escaped her. It washed warmly against his throat just seconds before she laved the leading edge of his collarbone with provocative, catlike strokes of her tongue. Reaction ripped through him, splintering his nerves and coiling the muscles in his large body.

He drew her up and into his arms, mindful of his lack of vision as he carefully took the final step to his bed. Once he bumped against it, he lowered Bliss onto the center of the mattress. He heard her whisper his name as he shed his pajama bottoms and followed her down onto the bed.

As he straddled her hips, he felt her place her hands atop his thighs, but he caught them and lifted them away from his body before she touched him. He felt like a rocket about to explode, and he knew the slightest contact would set him off. Leaning forward, he used a single fingertip to draw an invisible line from her naval up to the valley between her breasts. He traced the line a second time, but with his parted lips instead, his breath hot and moist as he nipped at her fragrant skin. He felt her shivery response, then circled the undersides of each plump breast with the tip of his tongue.

Bliss murmured his name, making it sound ever so precious as it spilled past her lips. As he crouched over her, she curved her hands around his shoulders. Micah cupped her breasts, his hands possessive as he claimed her as his own. She trembled, then went absolutely still. Despite his lack of vision, Micah recognized the tension-filled expectation that prompts a woman to hold her breath when she makes love with a man for the first time because she isn't completely certain of his intentions.

He stroked her with tenderness, determined to alleviate her anxiousness despite the desire that raged within him and made his fingers shake. Capturing one taut nipple between his teeth, Micah flicked his tongue back and forth across it, while simultaneously kneading her other breast. He tasted her, and he gloried in the salty-sweet flavor of her skin. Drawing her deeply into his mouth, he tortured her with his erotic sucking until she cried out her pleasure and bucked restlessly beneath him.

He taunted himself with vivid images of what it would be like once he buried his aching flesh inside her, just as he taunted her with sensation after sensation until her skin turned hot and damp. She muttered indecipherable words of encouragement, and for a while he forgot that he couldn't see her.

Micah's confidence soared as he savored her sounds of pleasure and the press of her fingers as she clutched at his shoulders. Shifting to her other breast, he began anew. Bliss responded as though she'd been struck by lightning. Her body quivered beneath his hands and mouth, and her back arched as she eagerly offered herself to him.

Her reaction, which seemed to embody an almost innocent sense of discovery and delight, fanned the flames of Micah's desire. Holding her made him feel as though he'd embraced an inferno. He worshiped her body, expressing physically the complex emotions cascading through him.

Passionately she chanted his name over and

over again, until it sounded like a mantra. He felt his body repeatedly tighten into itself as one violent rush of desire after another pummeled his senses. His inner tension mounted, threatening to overcome him, and his blood felt like a river of flame as it recklessly surged through his veins.

Micah finally paused, his breathing labored as he dragged air into and out of his lungs. Fighting yet again for control, he lowered his forehead to her breasts. A heartbeat later he felt the sweep of Bliss's fingertips as she stroked his nape.

Cupping his face between her hands, she urged him to lift his head with the slightest pressure of her palms. "You're fighting yourself, Micah—I can feel it. Trust what's happening between us. You don't have to be cautious with me."

He stopped breathing for a moment. His body stiffened, and his expression filled with wariness. He wondered if Bliss sensed his shock.

If she did, she ignored it. "The room is dark. You wouldn't be able to see me even if your eyes weren't bandaged. I meant what I said before. This isn't about seeing. It's about feeling, and you make me feel . . ." Her breath caught. She swallowed convulsively.

"You make me feel so much more than I've ever felt before."

"Do you have any idea what you do to me when I touch you?" Micah asked, his voice vulnerable, raw, and riddled with desire.

Instead of answering his question, she slipped her hands between their bodies and moved them slowly down the muscular length of his washboard-flat abdomen. She hesitated briefly when she reached his groin, then sank her fingers into the thatch of dense golden hair that surrounded his maleness.

Micah tensed, anticipating her next move. Her touch gentle but very delicate, Bliss closed her hands around the thick, pulsing strength of his arousal. Shock tremored through him, enflaming his senses with a wildly primitive sense of urgency.

She whispered, "I can feel exactly what I do to you."

He groaned, the sound that escaped him part humor at her unexpected boldness and part regret that he'd allowed his uncertainty to taint their intimacy. "I didn't want to rush you."

She laughed softly, shakily. "You couldn't. I've wanted this from the beginning, even though I wasn't about to admit it. Your ego doesn't need any nourishment."

Bliss stroked him intimately, as if to emphasize her sincerity. Micah surged within her hands, then groaned with disbelief. She was such a unique combination of seduction, innocence, and honesty that she stole away his breath and his wits each time she touched him.

"See me with your heart, Micah. No man should ever look at a woman in any other way when he makes love to her."

Hoarsely he confessed, "Whenever I think you've run out of surprises, you manage to come up with another one."

"I may be a little nervous and far less experienced than other women you've known, but I'm not less eager."

He tenderly cupped her face and sampled the flavors and textures of her mouth as he moved over her, his heart nearly bursting with the emotions she evoked. He tasted the eagerness she'd confessed, but he tasted and felt something even more profound as she returned his passion.

She was, he'd already concluded, a complex woman who trusted her instincts even as she allowed her heart to guide her through uncharted emotional terrain. By making herself vulnerable to intimacy and responsive to his needs, she was also, he sensed, making a statement about the feelings she harbored for him. Humbled by her emotional candor, he realized, not for the first time, that she was a woman who deserved to be cherished.

Lifting her arms, Bliss drew him even closer. Micah's thoughts scattered. His confidence flourished even as his body thrummed with heightened desire. He kept their hungry mouths fused as he leaned forward, using his arms to brace the weight of his upper torso, and aligned their bodies.

Bliss parted her thighs, her responsiveness nearly as shattering in its simplicity as her breathlessly whispered "Yes, Micah."

As he settled atop her, Micah's lean, hard body rippled with escalating tension. He felt stretched to the limit of his endurance as he absorbed the lush beauty of her taut-nippled breasts, the sleek contours of her firm belly, the cradling welcome of her upper thighs, and the smoothness of her skin as she circled his hips with her slender legs. She moved against him, the subtle uptilt of her pelvis devastating and utterly seductive.

"Come inside me," she begged as she nuzzled his neck with soft kisses. After skimming her fingertips up and down his muscular back, Bliss curved her hands over his narrow hips and urged him even nearer. "Feel for yourself what you've done to me, Micah. Feel *me*, and forget everything else."

He inhaled sharply, her invitation more arousing than any seduction he'd ever experienced. He shifted his hips, his straining manhood poised at the gate of her femininity. Lowering his head, he reclaimed her mouth. He kissed her, a hard, hot, and thoroughly intrusive kiss that matched the thrusting force of his loins as he surged into the heart of her passion. She cried out, the sound replete with relief and pleasure and shock as he buried his throbbing sex to the hilt.

One shudder after another racked his frame. His male instincts urged him to drive them both immediately into the arms of sensual oblivion, but because of his size, Micah forced himself to still his movements. He knew intuitively that Bliss needed time to adjust to the depth of his penetration. Slick, hot, and tighter than any woman he'd ever known, she felt almost like a virgin. He thanked God that she wasn't, because he doubted that he possessed the patience to treat her as one.

She tensed beneath him, her breathing shallow and her body trembling uncontrollably even as it sheathed him. Tilting her head back, she exhaled shakily as she sank her fingers into his tight buttocks. He framed her face with his hands, the last remnants of his restraint apparent as he gently kneaded her warm scalp.

She sighed, then shifted experimentally, cautiously. He felt relieved that her body was starting to recover from the shock of his entry. He ground his teeth together as she grew braver, and he felt as though he'd immersed himself in a steaming cauldron of wet silk. Her delicate inner muscles quivered around his maleness, and his erotic fantasies, which he'd indulged in each night until he thought he risked going mad from them, suddenly became a stunning reality.

His nerves felt shredded as he slowly dipped in and out of her body, pacing himself as he felt the ebb and flow of her delicate flesh around his manhood. Patience he didn't know he possessed allowed Micah to find his voice and the strength to use it. "Better now?" he asked.

She moaned. "Perfect."

The amazement he heard in her voice moved him in ways he hadn't imagined possible, especially for a jaded man who'd been at home in boudoirs around the globe. Realizing just how much she trusted him, he felt his heart constrict almost painfully in his chest.

"Micah, I have a confession to make."

He gathered her close. "I'm listening."

"This is only my second time. I didn't tell you before, because I didn't want to worry you."

He adored her, despite his shock, and he realized how easy it would be to fall in love with her if it weren't for the circumstances that presently controlled his life. Casting aside the uneasiness that came with this last troubling thought, Micah focused his attention on Bliss and tested her resilience with short, sharp strokes.

She came alive beneath him a heartbeat later, reminding him of a brilliant starburst. Her response was explosive as she undulated beneath him and her body adapted to the rhythm of his deepening strokes until he could think of nothing but the turbulent give and take of heated flesh. His good intentions about being the perfect lover flew out the window, to be replaced by one goal—the driving need for completion within Bliss's body. Nothing else mattered.

He wanted her so badly that he felt insane with desire. The clasp of her body resembled a tight fist, and he shuddered as she lifted her hips to meet the surging power of his sex. He drove into her again and again, the feel of her legs curved over his hips, her heels digging into the backs of his thighs, and her arms circling his shoulders intensifying his need even more. A sensual storm consumed them as Micah slid his hands down her back to her hips, his fingers pressing almost hurtfully into her skin as he held her and repeatedly, relentlessly thrust into her quivering depths.

He felt the change in her the instant it began, and he pushed her even harder, though he already teetered on the brink of climax him-

self. She surrendered totally to his demand,
keeping pace, matching him thrust for thrust,
sucking at his tongue with a ravenous mouth
even as her feminine sheath sucked at his hard
flesh.

Micah sensed the urgency that claimed her
when he felt her insides swell and quicken. He
heard, too, the start of a low moan in her
throat. Holding her close, he rode her hard,
forcing her into the almost savage prelude to
completion that only lovers ever truly understand. She writhed under him, her pelvis jerking sharply, her limbs tremoring with tension,
and her nails scoring his shoulders as she
clutched at him. His name burst past her lips,
the sound an odd blend of desperation and
panic.

Micah finally grasped the truth of her near-
frantic quest. She'd never known genuine
satisfaction before. His own inner tension escalating beyond his control, he felt compelled
to give her the fulfillment she deserved. He
thrust deeply enough to touch her soul, then
rocked from side to side before thrusting even
more deeply.

Bliss gasped, suddenly stiffened, then
started to convulse around him. He took her
scream of shocked pleasure into his mouth,
drinking it in, savoring it until he felt intoxi-
cated.

His lungs burned as he plunged into her over and over again. A second explosive climax seized her just moments later, the erotic milking of her quaking inner body too intense and far too provocative for Micah to resist. She triggered his release, which felled him like a blow from an iron fist and sent him spinning into a free-fall of sensation. He willingly succumbed to the mind-shattering force of the experience. With his own hoarse cry of pleasure echoing in his ears, Micah finally saw Bliss with his heart just seconds before his body exploded and he spent himself within her.

He collapsed atop her, feeling ripped to shreds and barely aware that her breathing was as ragged as his. She clung tightly to him, her arms locked around him and her face buried in the corded curve of his neck as aftershocks rumbled through her slender body. Micah soothed her with gentle hands and tender kisses. He discovered with no small amount of surprise that every tremor that passed through her body and every twitch of her delicate inner muscles simply served to revitalize his arousal.

Certain that he was probably crushing her with his weight, he finally heaved himself onto his side. He took her limp body with him in a tight embrace, aware that she needed time to recover even though he would have gladly inflamed her passion once again.

Sweat covered them both, but neither noticed or cared. Their bodies still intimately joined, Micah held Bliss while she dozed. He eventually relaxed enough to close his eyes and join her in sleep.

Bliss came awake slowly. Disoriented at first, she had no idea of the time. Although the near-darkness of the room contributed to her momentary confusion, the hard warmth of Micah's broad chest beneath her cheek and the steady cadence of her heartbeat assured her that she was where she belonged. She opened her eyes, focusing her thoughts, and a sense of well-being flooded her consciousness.

Sprawled lazily atop Micah's body, Bliss felt the glide of his hands down her back and across her hips. She sighed, her heart tripping quickly beneath her ribs, and her thighs parting in instinctive welcome. She registered the hard ridge of flesh trapped between their loins in the same instant that she felt his fingers dip into the dark cleft that concealed her feminine secrets. He stroked her, exploring the soft, moist folds of flesh with care until she trembled from his touch.

"Please don't stop," she whispered as she raised up a few inches and leaned forward.

He didn't. If anything, he intensified the

intimacy of their contact when he delved into her body with one long finger. She shifted higher up his body, but their connection remained unbroken as he followed her movement. She moaned softly, her pleasure a rich, earthy sound as she undulated sensuously atop him. Her breasts swayed against him, her sensitive nipples dragging across his coarse chest hair and tightening almost instantly. Her entire body began to feel like a chorus of colliding sensations, and she savored every one of them.

She wanted Micah's mouth at her breasts, but she didn't know how to tell him, so she left her need unvoiced. Pressing her lips to his temple, she trailed a line of kisses down the side of his face. The stubbly surface of his beard felt overtly erotic, and she shivered with the pleasure that rippled deep in her belly.

"I want you again," Micah growled as he clasped her waist, shifted her even higher up his body, and brought his lips to her breasts.

She arched like a cat as he took a nipple into the heat of his mouth, grateful that he'd recognized her need without being asked. Suspended over him, Bliss quivered as he used his teeth and swirling tongue on her. Pleasure oozed through her veins like a spill of hot honey, saturating her senses. She felt as though he intended to devour her, and she loved the idea that Micah was so hungry for her again. She ached inside, her body so aroused already that anticipation flowed through her like electrical currents.

"You want me too."

"Am I that obvious?" she asked shakily.

"You're that responsive."

Bliss smiled, confidence flowering inside her. "I'm glad you approve."

She caressed his cheek, the dim glow from a shaft of moonlight allowing her to study him as her gaze traveled over his hard features and then lingered at the patches of white gauze that covered his eyes. For his sake she wished he could see. For her sake she felt a kind of guilty relief that he couldn't, because then he would discover how desperately she loved him. She knew that one look at her expressive face would reveal the truth.

He pressed a kiss into the palm of her hand. "Why so quiet all of a sudden?" he asked as he draped her atop the muscular length of his body and anchored her hips with his hands.

"I don't know what to say. This is all so new."

"Then just feel," Micah urged, turning her words around and using them on her. With that piece of advice and without any warning, he flipped her onto her back, knelt between her thighs, and surged into her. He grinned. At her surprise, she decided.

"I couldn't wait."

Her breath caught. "I'm glad," she admitted, her amazement blending with wave after wave of sensation that rolled over her like an advancing tide.

Her eyes fluttered closed, but she opened them almost immediately when she felt Micah slide his hands beneath her thighs and lift her legs. She watched, startled and fascinated, as he hiked them over his shoulders, cupped her hips, and then shuddered almost violently as her flesh embraced him even more snugly.

She groaned throatily, so deep, so incredibly complete, was his penetration. She suddenly realized that she couldn't move. All she could really do was feel, and what she felt was beyond coherent description.

He didn't rush her, and for that she was grateful. Clasping her hips, Micah rocked against her, the slow, steady rhythm enticing and shockingly erotic. He let the pressure within her build at a languorous pace, teaching her in the process that while lovemaking could be violently explosive, it could also be the tenderest experience a man ever shared with a woman.

Exposed and vulnerable, Bliss felt the pressure of his rigid length right down to her soul. Micah smoothed one of his hands over her belly, tangling his fingers in the silk that shielded her secrets just seconds after she realized that she needed him to touch her there.

She held her breath, then nearly screamed with shock as he nuzzled the hidden bud of sensitivity with his knuckles. She bucked against him, her insides quivering violently around him. He caressed her with his thumb, his fingers fanning over her lower abdomen. She gasped and reached for him.

"Trust me, Bliss."

"I do! Oh God, I do." Her hands fell limply to her sides.

He shifted forward suddenly, but he didn't increase his pace. He kept pumping slowly into her, filling her, then withdrawing, then filling her again. Bliss felt utterly plundered by his gentle seduction. She also felt an inner strain that she recognized this time, a breathless spiraling tension that built inside her body until she wanted to scream. She trembled instead. Her hands found his shoulders as he leaned forward and laved her stomach with his hot tongue. Her fingers dug into his skin.

"Micah?"

"Slowly, Bliss. We're going to do this very slowly."

"You're driving me . . . I need . . ." Tears trickled from her eyes and back across her temples.

He lingered over her, driving into her with

deliberately deep, deliberately slow strokes, but she felt his escalating tension too. Relieved when he shifted her legs off his shoulders, she used them to snare his hips the instant he moved over her. She felt his hands skim up to her breasts, his fingers leaving little flashfires in their wake.

Still he refused to accelerate the measured pace of his loins. Desperate, Bliss clasped his head, guiding him so that she could claim his mouth. She explored him, tasting the sultry flavors of his sensuality as she frantically surged against him.

Only then did he give her what she craved. Only then did he unleash the power of his passion. Micah plunged smoothly, quickly. She felt as though he'd flipped a switch deep inside her. She called his name as she started to spin out of control. Clinging to him, Bliss realized that the summit she sought was within her grasp.

Her body quaked, and her insides clenched spasmodically. She splintered suddenly, a mindless, delirious pleasure lancing through her. Even as Bliss dissolved around Micah, she heard the moan that escaped him and inhaled it until it, and he, became an intrinsic part of her soul.

She spoke her love for him with her undulating body and stroking hands as he sought his own release. When his back arched, she felt his powerful frame tighten into itself. Bliss held Micah close to her heart, love swelling within her as he shuddered violently and then succumbed to the jetting force of a climax that eventually sent him sprawling across her.

EIGHT

Although groggy from sleeping so soundly, Bliss immediately realized that she was alone. She opened her eyes, surprised to find herself in her own bed, but also appreciative that Micah had thought to protect her from gossip by the housekeeping staff. As she sat up, she stretched and then glanced at her bedside clock, which confirmed that it was almost noon.

Freeing her legs from the tangle of sheets, Bliss left her bed and headed for the bathroom. She stood under the spray of a warm shower, her body feeling achy but gloriously replete after her night in Micah's arms. Even though she wondered about his mood and his thoughts this morning, she tried not to dwell on the emotional uncertainty she felt as she soaped and rinsed her body. Instead, she replayed in her mind the sensuality and passion they'd shared until exhaustion had claimed them shortly before dawn.

After drying her hair, Bliss dressed in a silk caftan and sandals, made her way to the kitchen, and while she drank a glass of juice she learned from one of the security guards that Captain Holbrook had been observed entering her studio a short while earlier. Her shock eclipsed her curiosity about whether or not he grasped the extent to which he'd altered the course of her life.

Bliss found the door to her studio wide open. Pausing on the threshold, she gave her eyes a moment to adjust from bright sunlight to the muted lighting of the cavernous, temperature-controlled room that housed the sculptures she'd just completed. She spotted Micah after she blinked a few times.

He was clad in his usual beach uniform of shorts, an abbreviated T-shirt, and athletic shoes. She concluded from the towel draped around his neck that he'd gone for a run after carrying her to her room. Bliss moved soundlessly into the studio's interior, her gaze captured by the look of concentration on Micah's face as he discovered with his fingertips the sweeping lines of the sculpture she'd finished just hours before his arrival at Rowland House.

A sensual, life-size work of a nude reclining in the surf, its impressionistic theme matched that of the other pieces in the collection, which were atop individual movers' dollies and lined up along the wall. Soon to be packed off to the New York gallery that handled her shows, the collection reflected her evolution as an artist.

She watched Micah linger over the sculpture. Bliss wondered if she'd captured his imagination with the work. She hoped so, because she wanted him to understand what no one else had ever grasped about her. Her creativity wasn't just a critical facet of her personality; it was an outlet—her only one until Micah—for her deeply passionate nature.

She heard him exhale heavily. Confused by the dispirited sound, she watched him withdraw his hand, turn, and extend the walking stick she'd given him. He moved forward, his normally confident expression marred by the frown on his face.

Bliss selected that moment to announce her presence. She walked toward him, no longer attempting to muffle the sound of her footsteps on the concrete floor of the studio. Her gaze darted to the bust she'd done of him, which was still situated atop a rotating pedestal in the center of the elongated room.

She felt uneasy about the outcome if he discovered the piece, explored it, and happened to recognize himself. Although she felt somewhat cowardly, she realized that she wasn't ready to explain the emotions that had compelled her to fashion his likeness in clay.

Micah paused, indicating his knowledge that Bliss had joined him when he said, "These are extraordinary."

"Thank you."

"The clay practically breathes. That takes remarkable skill and talent."

She smiled as she came to a halt in front of him. "I've never completely understood how it happens, so I trust my instincts, let everything come together, and wind up producing what I see in my mind."

"I counted a dozen pieces along the wall."

"A year's worth of work," Bliss confirmed, still baffled by the hard expression on his face.

"Cyrus has several pieces."

Bliss looked startled. "He does?"

"In his office in Washington and in his home in Virginia."

"I haven't been to either location in several years."

"He's obviously an admirer."

Frowning, she admitted, "I gave him an early piece, but that was a long time ago." Silently she pleaded, Talk to me about last night, not about my father.

"He has an extensive collection, each piece unique in theme and style. I know because I've seen them. Cyrus refers to them as 'Elizabeth's creations.'"

"My real name," she said, suddenly aware that he recognized her true identity.

"Cyrus cares about you, Bliss."

But do you? she couldn't help wondering, her vulnerable emotions making her feel nervous and insecure. "I guess he must, given what you've just told me."

"He may not talk about you, but he wouldn't display your sculptures if he weren't proud of you."

"Why didn't he just ask me? He doesn't have to buy my work."

"Why didn't you just give them to him?" Micah countered in a voice that sounded as unforgiving as granite.

"I didn't think . . ." Was I really going to say I didn't think my father cared about the person I've become? she wondered, guilt coursing through her that she'd been so judgmental.

"Maybe you should."

"You're right. I *should* think. I've made assumptions about him for years, possibly incorrect assumptions."

"It's worth checking out." Micah turned, his instincts guiding him in such a way that Bliss got the impression he was actually studying the creations lined up along the wall. "I didn't expect all this."

"It's my work. It's a part of who I am."

"It's more than that, Bliss. Touching your sculptures is an intimate experience, almost like taking a stroll across your soul. I felt your passion and the vitality you naturally exude. They feel . . . alive."

She felt relieved that he understood. "I have a show in New York in a few weeks. I've spent the last year getting ready for it. The owner of the gallery that handles my work is sending down a special moving team. They'll crate everything and transport the sculptures so that they're properly arranged prior to my arrival."

"You're a very successful artist."

She thought she heard what sounded like distaste in his voice. A part of her resented him for it, but another part of her needed to understand his reaction. "Yes, but the art world's a quirky place. Artists can maintain a high profile for years on end, or they can suddenly fall out of favor with the critics. You have to decide whom you're creating for at the outset of your

career—the critics, the collectors, or yourself.
I've always opted for the latter."

Micah moved closer, his expression grim.
She glanced once more at the nearby pedestal,
and she knew in that instant that she'd captured
even the most subtle nuances of his character.
The only portion of the sculpture that had
required the use of her memory had been the
eyes, but she'd never forgotten the piercing
quality of his blue-eyed gaze or the slashing
drama of his dense golden eyebrows. She
doubted she ever would.

Bliss reached out and placed her palm
against his hard chest. She wanted to walk
straight into his arms and feel the strength of
his embrace, but she didn't. She sensed that
this wasn't the right time, even though she
didn't understand why.

"You should have told me."

Confused by his accusatory tone, she
peered up at him. "I did."

"*Time* and *People* have done articles about
you, although I don't recall ever seeing a pho-
tograph."

She shrugged as she withdrew her hand.
"I cherish my privacy. Besides, those maga-
zines do profiles of many artists. I'm hardly
unique."

He grasped her upper arm with his free
hand. "No, Bliss. They do profiles only of the

stars, the people who've reached the top in their artistic medium."

Bliss frowned. "Am I supposed to apologize for being celebrated? You're a legend in Naval Intelligence, and you certainly don't feel the need to apologize."

"I'm not asking for an apology."

"Then what do you want?"

"Nothing." He freed her. "Nothing at all."

Startled, she stepped back a pace and pressed her hands to her sides. "Micah, talk to me. Tell me what this is all about."

"You're way out of my league, lady."

"That's crazy. I'm the woman who just spent the night in your bed, the woman who made love with you until we both nearly collapsed, so quit treating me like a stranger you just met on the street. You're not being fair or kind."

"You're more than I . . ."

"I'm a woman, and you're a man. You happen to be a man with a vision problem, but I defy you to find a single person on this planet who isn't dealing with problems right this minute. You've helped me zero in on one of mine, for heaven's sake. You've also made me realize I haven't figured out how to have a relationship with my father, but that doesn't mean I'm going to jump off the nearest cliff. You've showed me that I need to work on rebuilding the trust I once had for him. Micah, we're all flawed, but that doesn't mean we can't care about each other."

"You don't understand."

"Obviously," she declared, a curious belligerence flaring within her. "After last night, I thought . . ."

He cut in, "I don't want to hurt your feelings."

Shock ricocheted through her. She felt as though he'd just slammed a fist against her chest. "You're sorry about last night," she whispered.

She abruptly turned away from him, unwilling to lose control of her emotions in front of him, but he stayed in range, grabbing her shoulder with his free hand and jerking her back to stand in front of him. She felt his fingers dig into her flesh, and she remembered the way he'd touched her, the forceful passion he'd exposed her to, the night before. Now, his touch felt cold, even angry.

"I'm not sorry, Bliss. I couldn't be sorry in a million years."

"Well, I'm not either," she said heatedly.

"Calm down."

"Don't give me orders."

"Fine. Have it your way."

He freed her, leaving her with the impression that he couldn't bear to touch her anymore. Her heart nearly stopped beating. She studied him, desperate to understand his motives.

"Micah, why are you being so difficult?"

"I'm being realistic." His grip on the walking stick tightened, and his chin rose. "My parents are equal partners."

Be patient with him, her emotions urged. "Most married people are if they have a good relationship," she reminded him gently.

"They aren't dependent on each other."

"How can you say that? People who love are always dependent and vulnerable. That's a part of loving and trusting another person." Because of the expression on his face, she quickly realized that her argument wasn't making a dent in his attitude. "Didn't you tell me your father has serious health problems, and that your mother's a nurse?"

"They're still equals in all the ways that count."

"So are we, Micah. You aren't being reasonable."

"He's not a burden," he muttered in a low voice she almost didn't hear.

"Well, neither are you, if that's what you're implying."

"I'm not implying. I'm stating the obvious, and I'm being realistic, for both our sakes."

"You're being ridiculous," she snapped,

unable to remain in control any longer. "Put aside your ego for a moment, and give me one example of when you think I've treated you like a burden."

"You haven't. I don't blame you for the way I feel."

"We could live as equals, if you'd let us. Trust yourself and trust us, or we're destined for failure."

Micah shook his head, moved past her, and strode out of the studio, his walking stick extended in front of him. Bliss stared after him, too shocked to move as she watched him disappear from sight.

Nearly blinded by the tears that filled her eyes, she approached the clay bust of Micah, slipped her arms around it, and hugged the unyielding surface. She wept, but only until her anger with the situation, and with Micah, resurfaced.

Bliss didn't linger in her studio. Instead of letting herself completely unravel, she decided to follow Micah. She doubted that he'd feel inclined to talk, but she suddenly didn't care. She knew they couldn't leave things the way they were. Too much had happened between them, and she reasoned that no matter how much inner conflict Micah felt about the success or failure of his surgery, he needed to understand that running away solved nothing.

Although she didn't expect a commitment or a declaration of love from him, she meant to persuade him to at least keep an open mind about their relationship and his future.

Making her way to Micah's suite, Bliss also realized that if she didn't fight for them now, she might never have the chance again. She knocked on his door, then let herself into his rooms without waiting for an invitation. She paused when she saw him. With his head bowed and shoulders slumped, he stood in the doorway that led out to their private patio. Bliss felt a twinge of despair as she remembered that their intimacy had begun on that same patio. At the moment, though, it was as though that had happened to two total strangers.

"I'm not accustomed to people walking out on me in the middle of a conversation," she began.

She saw him stiffen. When he didn't bother to turn around or respond to her remark, Bliss closed the space that separated them. Standing beside him, she glanced at his profile and registered the glacial expression on his face. She felt momentarily taken aback by the cold look, but she mustered the courage she needed to confront him and took a moment to collect her thoughts.

"Shall we try again, Micah?"

"There's no point. We have nothing to discuss."

"I feel as though you're turning your back on what we shared last night. It was a beginning, not some tawdry one-night stand. Making love with you meant the world to me, and I'm having a difficult time believing that you didn't place a high value on it too."

He turned and leaned back against the doorframe, but his facial expression remained empty of emotion. "Last night was a mistake. It won't happen again."

She stared at him for several moments while she gathered her wits and found a way to compartmentalize, if only for a short time, the hurt that he'd just inflicted. "I've never been called a mistake before, Micah. It's a new experience for me, and I'm not sure quite how to handle it."

He swore under her breath. "That's not what I said, and you know it."

"I know you feel at a disadvantage. I know you're angry about your eyes, but I also know how I felt when we made love, and I definitely remember what it was like each time you climaxed inside of me. Micah, we captured the very essence of life and hope when we held each other." Bliss paused and swallowed against the emotion rising up inside her. "I felt more than simple lust last night, and I'd swear you did too."

"Don't do this, Bliss," he warned, his tone guttural, his expression stone cold.

"Don't do what, Micah? Don't remember? Don't have feelings? Don't talk about how incredible we were together, because then you'll have to find a way past your damnable pride and think of someone other than yourself for a change?" She heard the strident sound of her voice and deliberately softened it. "Don't care about you?"

He walked away, his shoulder brushing against her as he moved past her. She steadied herself, keeping her gaze fastened on him. She took in the tension that infused his large-framed body with rigidity, and she felt a burst of compassion explode inside her.

Micah paused in the center of the room. He slowly pivoted until he faced her. "Don't punish either one of us with what might have been. Just get past it. You'll forget me once I'm gone."

"Explain to me how I could have misjudged you so completely," she challenged, reckless emotions displacing her compassion.

"There's nothing to explain, Bliss. The simple truth is that you deserve more than I can offer."

She calmed herself with great effort. "What

do I deserve?" she asked as she approached him.

"A real partner. Not a man who'd be dependent on you to be his eyes."

"If I were a nurse or a teacher or even a secretary, would you still feel the same way?"

He hesitated, then asked, "Does it matter?"

"Yes, Micah, so please answer the question."

He exhaled, the sound laden with what Bliss thought might be emotional fatigue. Although his silence wore on her nerves, she found the patience to wait for his reply.

"Probably. Maybe. Hell, I don't know. How can I know? You aren't any of those things. You're a celebrated sculptor. The sky's the limit for you, and no one should be allowed to stand in your way."

"How incredibly small-minded of you. You're actually penalizing me because I've made a name for myself, and the art world considers me a success."

"Don't twist my words, Bliss. You know what I'm saying."

"No, I don't think I do. Why don't you spell it out for me? I'm feeling particularly dense right now, and that's probably because I'm so furious with you."

"Listen to me," he ordered sharply. "Last

night was a fantasy, not the beginning of anything remotely meaningful. My life's a washout. I may never see again. I can't offer you anything other than sex. If that's enough, then say so, and we'll figure things out from there."

"Sex? You're offering me stud service, is that it? How generous!" she exclaimed. She felt rage and pain coalesce in her heart until the combination of negative emotions threatened to strangle her. "You know, I'm starting to feel like the sap who gets the joke prize at a gift exchange. You gave me joy and hope and love last night, but now you're taking it all back, aren't you?"

"Get out of here, Bliss. I'm not offering you a thing, not even sex." He shoved his fingers through his pale hair, then brought his hand to his side and closed it into a fist. "I meant what I said earlier. What happened last night was a mistake, and it won't happen again, so please leave me alone. There's nothing left to say."

"I cannot believe this is happening to us," she whispered, all the fight and fury suddenly draining out of her.

"Believe it, lady, and get on with your life."

Bliss somehow managed to make her way to her own suite. Sinking down onto the edge of her bed, she covered her face with her hands and rocked back and forth. She couldn't cry, even though she wanted to. Nor could she resummon her anger with Micah, although she wished she could. She felt too drained and too numb for even the most straightforward of emotions.

Stretched out atop her bed and hugging her pillow, Bliss drifted mentally, periodically dozing as she tried to pull herself back together.

A sharp series of knocks roused her from her lethargy later that afternoon. Bliss forced herself to her feet and swiped at her wrinkled clothes. Stumbling to the door, she pulled it open, expecting to find a member of the household staff in the hallway. Stunned by the identity of the person who stood before her, she gaped at her unexpected visitor.

"You look like hell. Are you ill?" Cyrus Rowland demanded.

Too surprised to respond, Bliss moved out of her father's way as he strode into her suite, glanced around, and then walked to the French doors and threw them open. "What's going on? Micah's behaving like a bee-stung jackass, and you look like you've just endured a forced march. I thought you said things were going well down here when we talked a few days ago."

She stiffened, but she kept her voice level as she spoke. "We've had a tough day, Dad. There's really no need to go into it right now."

He nodded. "Good. I need to make some

calls, so I'll be in the library for a few hours. We'll have cocktails at six, then dinner at the Lagoon at seven-thirty. Micah's joining us."

Her father paused in front of her. Bliss detected a hint of hesitancy in his manner, which surprised her. Although she didn't understand the curious look on his face, she felt a sense of resignation when he made no move to embrace her. Given the chance, she knew she would have sold her soul for a hug from him at that particular moment.

"You look pale," he observed, his hazel eyes narrowed and his voice unexpectedly subdued as he skimmed her features with a probing gaze. "Take better care of yourself in the future."

He didn't wait for a reply. Bliss stared after him as he strode out of her suite and down the hallway, her scrambled brain trying to digest his unannounced presence and his orchestration of the coming evening. She sighed, the heavy sound an accurate reflection of the defeat she felt. She'd lost control of her life, and she wondered if she'd ever get it back again.

Closing her bedroom door, Bliss pondered the wisdom of spending an evening with Micah and her father. As she stood beneath the shower a short while later, she concluded that a weekend in hell would be less stressful. She loved them both, although in vastly different ways, but neither one seemed to want her in his life. Once again Bliss recognized her role as an outsider. She truly felt like one, and she silently cursed the two men who'd made her feel this way.

NINE

Bliss exited the limo last. The security contingent remained alert but nonintrusive, as was their habit when protecting both her father and Micah. She appreciated their restraint and competence.

The restaurant owner, a man she'd known for many years, greeted them with enthusiasm, embracing Bliss after shaking hands with Cyrus and Micah, and escorted them inside to their table. Bliss knew they drew the attention of the other diners, but most were considerate local people who knew Cyrus Rowland by reputation and didn't begrudge him his need for armed protection.

Cyrus chatted easily once they were seated, pausing to order a bottle of wine that Bliss recalled as his favorite from a California vintner who also happened to be a longtime personal friend.

"You look lovely tonight, Bliss, very much like your mother when she was your age."

Clad in a deceptively casual-looking evening pantsuit of cream satin, Bliss concealed her surprise at his comment and thanked him. She glanced at Micah, who sat stiffly in his chair. Reaching out, she slipped his water glass to a position above his knife and spoon. She nearly jumped from her chair when his hand darted out and captured her wrist.

"The same position as at home?" he asked, his voice rife with tension.

She stared at him. *Home?* The word shocked her, especially since he often treated the Rowland House estate like a prison. "That's right."

While Micah retreated to silence and let Cyrus carry the conversation with amusing anecdotes about his most recent travels in the Orient on behalf of the president, Bliss empathized with Micah in his anxiety. This was his first meal in a restaurant. His distress, although hidden behind an expressionless facade, revived her instinctive compassion, and she consciously set aside her frustration with him.

"I've always enjoyed the menu here," she remarked once the headwaiter presented the wine selection to Cyrus for his inspection.

"The chef is excellent, even though he apparently runs the kitchen like a tyrant. From what I understand, he trained and worked in Paris. I can't ever decide what to order, the crab-stuffed shrimp, the veal piccata, or the medallions of beef with either a hollandaise or a wine sauce."

She felt the press of her father's gaze and looked questioningly at him. His approving nod caught her by surprise, and she started to wonder about his state of mind. She couldn't ever recall a time when he'd behaved with such overt approval of her behavior.

A second waiter arrived shortly after the wine was poured. Bliss listened as Micah used the cues she'd given him and ordered his meal. A few minutes later she felt her heart swell with pride when a well-known politician and his wife stopped at their table to exchange a few words. Micah set aside his napkin, got to his feet, and extended his hand when introduced to the senator and his lady.

If Micah felt less than secure about observing the social amenities, Bliss saw no sign of hesitation or self-doubt in his demeanor. He remained on his feet until the couple departed, reclaiming his chair with a confident manner and a physical grace that Bliss had come to appreciate in him. Only when he located his wineglass with shaking fingers did she fully grasp the depth of his inner tension.

She wanted to slip her arms around him and tell him how wonderfully he'd handled what could have been an awkward situation, but she sensed that he already knew it. Although she felt protective of him, she didn't intend to compromise his dignity.

Bliss managed to relax enough to answer several questions put to her by her father about her upcoming New York show. She wondered if he was trying to distract her from worrying about Micah. Without appearing to break stride as she listened to her father, she noted in quiet asides to Micah the arrangement of the food on his plate with each course that was served.

Mellow-sounding music by a popular Saint Thomas band drifted around them. Bliss had always considered the band's sound uniquely sensual and very appropriate for the lovers who frequented the Lagoon. As her gaze strayed to Micah as he responded to a remark from Cyrus, she was unaware that her love for him glowed in her green almond-shaped eyes.

Cyrus filled in the few conversational lapses that occurred as they dined. He responded with unusual animation whenever Bliss asked a question. She felt grateful for his obvious willingness to make the evening a positive experience for Micah, even though she couldn't completely conceal her amazement that he managed the task with such ease.

This, she realized, was a side of her father that she'd rarely seen during their infrequent visits since the divorce. She decided, without any resentment, that his fondness for Micah had allowed him to display the amiable personality normally hidden beneath layers of professional preoccupation.

Micah concentrated on his meal, although he tasted little of what he consumed. After finishing his food and placing his silverware on the outside rim of his plate, he stiffened, his head tilting to one side as he heard the garbled sound of a voice coming from a two-way radio. A few seconds later he heard unfamiliar footsteps on the hardwood floor. Instincts too ingrained to ignore alerted him to the presence of an individual other than a member of the restaurant staff.

"Cyrus, behind you." Micah spoke tersely, startling Bliss with his abrupt comment and drawing a smile from his former boss.

"It's Hamilton, son, the new Secret Service fellow I told you about this afternoon." Cyrus glanced at Bliss, a satisfied, pride-filled smile on his face. "Hamilton has heavy feet."

Confused, she repeated, "Heavy feet?"

Cyrus chuckled. "Micah notices things that

everyone else seems to miss. He kept me out of harm's way once when he realized that a man disguised in a U.S. Army uniform was actually a Middle East terrorist on a suicide mission meant to take out an entire diplomatic team. All because the fellow had an uneven gait and his shoes made the wrong sound when he traversed a stretch of corridor in the embassy."

Micah shrugged, uncomfortable with Cyrus's praise. He knew that if a life-threatening situation occurred now, he'd be virtually useless. In order to keep Cyrus from speaking at length about the past, he said, "The leather soles of American-made shoes have a distinctive sound. I imagine it has something to do with the density of the leather. Military men tend to walk in a certain way, and there's rarely any hesitation in their stride when they're on familiar terrain."

Hamilton, a pale young man with a damp upper lip, a nervous manner, and darting eyes, leaned down next to Cyrus. "Excuse me, sir. You have a call from the White House. I have a secure phone ready for your use in the manager's office."

Cyrus left his chair with obvious reluctance. "This may take some time. Why don't you two go ahead with dessert?"

"I'm impressed," Bliss admitted once

Cyrus and Hamilton departed the dining room.

"Don't be. It was my job for over fifteen years." He fell silent as their waiter served coffee and snifters of cognac.

"You still do it very well," she observed, her voice subdued but firm.

He flinched, then carefully located his coffee cup and saucer. He said nothing in response to her remark. Instead, he placed his palm about an inch above the rim of his cup, as Bliss had taught him to in order to test the degree of heat in a hot beverage. "Wait on the coffee," he suggested, not even considering the proprietary tone of his voice as he spoke to Bliss. "It won't be drinkable for a few minutes."

"You're doing fine this evening," she said.

"You're not," Micah returned bluntly. "You sound like a rubber band that's been stretched too tight. You're about to snap inside."

"Micah . . ."

"Who's doing the best job of making you uncomfortable? Me or your father?"

"I'm not uncomfortable," she insisted.

He gripped his coffee cup with both hands. "Don't lie to me, Bliss."

"My father has been remarkably relaxed and charming this evening, so I haven't any complaints about his behavior, but I am still angry with you about this afternoon."

He knew he should have been accustomed to her honesty by now, but it startled him. "I didn't want to hurt you, but I did anyway."

"Can't we talk about what's happened between us?"

As he cast about mentally for a way to distract her, Micah seized on the first idea that popped into his mind. "The band's pretty good. Is there a dance floor?"

"Of course."

"Is it crowded?" If they were going to dance, he didn't want to risk crashing into people he didn't know. Although he doubted the wisdom of trying to navigate a dance floor without being able to see his surroundings, he realized that he would risk almost any humiliation in order to hold Bliss in his arms again.

"There are only two couples out there. There's plenty of space."

Micah frowned. He thought he heard eagerness in her voice. In the next instant he told himself that he was imagining things in order to salve his own ego. He pushed himself to his feet and extended his hand in her direction. "Let's try it then, if you don't mind a mashed toe or two."

Her fragrance, which he inhaled as she stood and moved to stand beside him, stimulated his senses. He clamped down on his response to her, the muscles in his body tremoring with suppressed tension. The feel of her slender fingers as she slid her hand into his eased his anxiety about making a fool of himself in a public place, but only fractionally. He remembered too well what her evocative touch had done to him the previous night.

Micah adapted his long-legged stride to Bliss's shorter one, and they made it to the dance floor without incident. When she slipped into his arms, she reminded him of a conclusion he'd reached about her the night before. They fit together, despite the disparity in their sizes. Had fate been less harsh, he realized that he would have claimed this woman as his own for the rest of his life.

"I can think of only one other thing I'd enjoy more than dancing," she said softly.

"What's that?"

She edged closer, her breasts brushing, then nestling against, his broad chest and sending a riot of sensation into his bloodstream. "Making love with you."

He nearly stumbled. Since he already felt like an ass for the way he'd treated her, he excused her deliberately provocative remark. He loved her, but he refused to consider saddling her with his problems, no matter how willing she seemed to take them on.

Micah registered with his senses the proximity of the other couples on the dance floor, and he knew they could see the bandages that covered his eyes. As a result, they were obviously willing to give him a wide berth. Although he resented the need, his confidence flourished, in large part, he realized, because of Bliss's ability to follow his lead. They danced for a long time, the music a sultry counterpoint to the seductive sensations stirring Micah's blood and threatening to blister his veins.

"I love being in your arms," Bliss murmured.

He inhaled sharply. "Don't do this."

"You're not under any obligation, Micah."

Her remark did nothing to lessen the arousal storming his senses and coiling his muscles into snug knots. If anything, he felt even more inclined to take her right where they stood.

"This isn't quite as good as making love, is it? I want the intimacy back, Micah, at least until you leave."

Although he recognized the courage it took for her to make such a statement, he harshly warned, "We can't, so drop the subject right now."

She ignored his order, her voice like hot silk as she said, "You wouldn't be using me, if that's what's troubling you. I'd accept you on your terms."

"If you don't call it using, then what the hell would it be?" he demanded.

"Sharing? Trusting our emotions? Stealing a little more happiness?" She hesitated, then taunted him with the sensual shift of her hips against his swollen loins. "I know you want me. I can feel exactly how much you want me."

He jerked at the contact. "Damnit to hell, Bliss," he growled. Shuddering, he tightened his arms around her until their bodies seemed to be forged together. He smothered a groan even as he hungered to fit himself into the welcoming cradle of her thighs.

"Your body doesn't lie, Micah. Neither does mine. I'm simmering inside, and you're the cause."

"This is tough enough. Don't make it worse."

"I want to make it better, but I can't do it alone," she whispered. "Help me. Meet me halfway."

His fingers spasmed, digging into her narrow waist before he released her and seized her hand. "Let's go back to our table. Cyrus is probably ready to leave by now."

"So much for my powers of seduction," she muttered to herself as they rejoined her father. As Micah predicted, Cyrus had already settled the bill in anticipation of their departure. Bliss numbly collected her purse, thanked the restaurant owner for his hospitality and the fine meal, and preceded Micah and Cyrus to the waiting limo.

"I'm sorry we had to cut our evening short, but I have to go over some paperwork before I return to Washington in the morning," Cyrus explained as they walked into the foyer of Rowland House twenty minutes later.

"I'll be flying back to Washington with you, sir."

Bliss gripped her evening bag with both hands, quelling the cry of dismay that welled up inside her. She felt her father's questioning gaze, but she feared revealing the emotions threatening to choke her if she risked speaking, so she remained silent.

Cyrus frowned, but he nodded. "There'll be a helicopter on the front lawn at zero six hundred hours, son."

"I'll be ready. Thank you for dinner. Good night, Bliss." Micah crossed the foyer, his footsteps fading as he made his way to his suite.

Bliss felt as though she'd taken a fierce blow to the body. Raising her chin a notch and fighting tears, she looked at her father. The compassion and pity she saw in his eyes almost made her weep because his response was so unexpected.

"Do you have a moment, Bliss?"

"Certainly." She followed him into the library, watching as he sank into a chair and withdrew one of his trademark cigars from the inside pocket of his suit jacket.

"He's worth your effort."

"I don't know what you mean."

"Of course you do."

She felt the dam that contained her fragile emotions collapse inside her. "Only a fool tries to force another person to love them," she blurted out.

"You aren't a fool, Bliss, and I don't think I've ever known a more honorable man than Micah Holbrook. Unfortunately he lets his pride get in his way when he shouldn't."

"Why did you send him to *me*?" She didn't try to hide the faintly bitter tone in her voice.

"He needed you. I think you need him, too, don't you?"

"Matchmaking, Dad?"

"Perhaps, but only subconsciously."

"I love him, but he doesn't want me."

"Do you really think he knows what he wants right now?"

She swiped at the tears that spilled from her eyes. "He believes he does."

"I thought I knew what I wanted a long time ago, too, but I didn't. I let my pride and my ambition destroy my marriage to your mother.

I didn't make allowances for her needs, and I failed her even when I knew she was dying."

She saw his regret and realized with a start how genuine it was. "You were divorced. Your lives had gone in different directions."

"My mistake, Bliss, and I regret it."

"Why *did* you divorce? I never really understood, and no one would tell me when I asked."

"I loved her too much when I was a young man. I wanted her, but I felt inadequate in her sophisticated world, so I decided to carve out my own place in the world of foreign affairs. I've achieved most all of my goals, but I did it at her expense. I also hurt her deeply with behavior that was . . . inappropriate for a married man, and she left me."

"Mother always loved you, even at the end," Bliss assured him. "Your name was on her lips when she died."

Clearly stunned, Cyrus left his chair and walked to the marble fireplace. Bliss watched him stare at the empty grate for several minutes before she approached him and put her hand on his shoulder. "Thank you for being honest with me, Dad."

He turned, tucking his unlighted cigar into the breast pocket of his suit, and studied her, his expression that of a man still wrestling with his emotions. "I care about you too. I just don't always know how to show it."

"Micah helped me realize something important about the gulf between us. I've judged you by my expectations, which hasn't really been fair to you."

"You had every right to judge me. I've failed you in so many ways during your life."

She took an uneven breath. "I want my father back. Is there room for me in your busy world?"

"I want my daughter, so I'll make room," Cyrus declared gruffly.

She slipped into his arms when he extended them, the cigar-scented warmth of a fatherly embrace something she'd yearned for nearly all of her life.

Wiping away her tears, Bliss smiled up at him a few moments later. "And no more buying my sculptures," she scolded. "From now on you'll receive one piece from every collection. A gift from your daughter, because she loves you."

"Promise me that you'll try to give Micah a second chance too. Once he realizes what he's lost, he'll be back."

She paled, then nodded.

TEN

Bliss spent the next few hours alone in her suite. Still reeling from the emotional roller-coaster ride of the last twenty-four hours, she worked at coming to terms with the turnaround in her relationship with her father and her increasingly conflicted feelings concerning the gulf that now separated her from Micah.

She felt both grateful and oddly strengthened by her conversation with Cyrus, and from that strength, not just her conviction that she and Micah deserved one last night together, she found the courage to set aside her own wounded pride and go to him.

She slipped into his suite through the unlocked patio doors. She didn't let herself hope that Micah had deliberately left the doors unsecured, although she wanted to. After closing them, Bliss walked barefoot across the spacious, moonlight-flooded room. She felt certain that Micah sensed her presence, even though he failed to acknowledge her.

With her heart hammering wildly in her chest, she paused in the center of the room, slid the straps of her nightgown off her shoulders, and let the gown slip free of her body. Naked, she stepped out of the puddle of black lace, her gaze fixed on Micah as she approached him.

He sat with his back against the headboard. His broad shoulders and chest were bare, a light cotton sheet draped over his long legs and hips.

Bliss thought about her behavior on the dance floor earlier that evening. She wondered if Micah considered her brazen, but she decided that it would be foolish to apologize for expressing her feelings and needs. If anything, she almost wished that she'd said more, even though she wasn't altogether sure what that "more" could have been. She knew her limited experience with men didn't exactly lend itself to world-class seductions.

Bliss paused at the end of the king-sized bed. "Are you going to turn me away, Micah?"

Silence stretched tautly between them. She remained motionless, the nerve endings within her body tingling with anticipation, her breasts swelling and her nipples tightening to pebble-hardness because she craved Micah's touch and the feel of his aroused flesh surging into her own. The strangling hand of fear clasped her heart while she waited, her patience fraying even more with each passing second, for Micah to respond.

"We both know I should, Bliss."

Her heart leapt into her throat. He hadn't asked her to leave. Despite his somberly spoken words, she knelt between his parted ankles. She said nothing as she closed her hands over the rumpled sheet that covered the bottom half of his long, lean body.

"Because you don't want me?" she whispered.

"Because I *do* want you."

She gripped the fabric, her gaze fastened on his features as she tugged at the sheet. She watched a muscle tick violently in his clenched jaw and saw his head tilt slightly to the right, as though he meant to study her even if he couldn't see her. She held her breath and slowly moved the sheet downward, inch by agonizing inch, despite her inner need to wrench the material free of him and force him to acknowledge his need of her once and for all.

Micah halted the progression of the sheet while it still covered his loins, his hands fisted into the fabric on either side of his hips.

Bliss pulled once more, desire and determination flowing like heated currents through her bloodstream. She heard the hiss of a curse, the word indistinct but replete with frustration, frustration she grasped because she understood this complex man and the pride within him that prevented him from admitting his need. She realized that because he believed that his ability to control his destiny had been taken from him, he now fought to control his response to her.

"I belong to you tonight if you want me, Micah. No conditions and no false promises. Don't deny either one of us."

He groaned and opened his hands. She yanked the fabric free, revealing the power of his jutting manhood, his narrow hips, and the muscular strength of his hair-dusted thighs. She felt a corresponding groan of response thrum soundlessly through her own body. It produced a simmering heat that stole through her veins and a moistening sensation that hinted at molten potential.

She trembled, eyeing him cautiously as he leaned back and rested his head against the top edge of the headboard. The ragged sigh that escaped him tore at her heart, and she finally realized that he was trying to be noble, not stubborn or cruel. She loved him even more for the inner battle he waged, but she didn't intend for him to win. Not this time.

"Come here, Bliss," he groaned.

She shook her head. "Not yet." She shoved the sheet aside, her gaze traveling feverishly over the length and breadth of his muscular body.

"You win," he conceded. "I'll admit that I want you."

"We both win, because I want you, too, but first I need to touch you, Micah. I need to memorize every inch of your body, and I don't want to miss a single detail, because it's all I'll have once you're gone."

He exhaled, the sound harsh as it broke free of him. He jerked a nod in her direction, and he remained in a half-reclining position against the headboard.

Bliss moved up his body like a slow, hot tide, tantalizing, enveloping, consuming. She started at his ankles, her fingertips gliding around them as though to measure their width. As she inched forward between his spread legs, she circled his well-developed calves, cupping the backs of them, her fingertips tracing the taut, muscled flesh that bunched beneath her hands. She shifted higher still, her fingertips skimming up and over his knees.

She taunted and she teased, exploring the musculature of his legs with love and with the ingrained instincts of a sculptor. She drove her fingers into the dense hair that covered his powerful thighs. The muscles beneath her palms and fingers flexed and flowed. She laughed, the low sound softly seductive and filled with pleasure.

"Talk to me," Micah ordered roughly. "What are you thinking?"

"I have this thing for your legs. I love watching you run. The muscles in your body move with absolute harmony."

"The muscles in my body are tied up in knots, thanks to you."

She slid her hands upward, the heat emanating from his skin almost scorching her fingertips. She felt the tension that made the muscles flutter above his groin just before she sifted her fingers through the nest of coarse hair that framed his maleness.

Micah sucked in his breath, then shuddered. He reached for her, but Bliss brushed aside his hands.

"Be patient," she whispered. She smoothed a finger over the tip of his manhood, which surged beneath her light touch. Bliss smiled, aroused even more by his response. "Each time I touch you, I feel the overwhelming desire to sculpt your shape."

"Is that all you feel?" he ground out through clenched teeth.

She clasped him with gentle, encompassing hands. The pulsing strength of his sex reminded her of the heart-stopping pleasures she'd experienced when their bodies had merged so many times the night before.

"No, Micah," she whispered. "That's not all."

She stroked him, her touch so erotic that he swelled to the point of bursting beneath her feathery exploration. Bliss felt as though she held a length of hot forged metal in her hands. Leaning down, she lightly swirled the tip of her tongue over his erection before she closed her mouth around him and tasted his essence.

Micah jerked under the wet heat of her mouth, his hips lifting off the bed with helpless spontaneity. Bliss felt his hands settle on her shoulders, his fingers spasming with a rhythm that felt gloriously possessive. She loved him then, bathing him in the fiery passion he'd inspired and saturating his senses with a profoundly erotic expression of her emotions in an act that she'd never considered sharing with any man but Micah.

He drove his fingers into the cap of curls that framed her features. "Bliss . . . "

She smiled at the sensual agony she heard in his voice. He'd made her feel just as out of control, so much so that she'd begged him for release. He'd given it to her, of course, but only when she'd thought that she would go mad from the sensual torture he'd inflicted on her.

Straightening several moments later, she shifted over him to straddle his thighs.

"You're driving me crazy," Micah accused.

"Aren't I supposed to?" she asked, playfully, dragging her knuckles across the muscles that ridged his belly.

"Yes. No. Hell, I haven't got a clue. I can't think straight right now."

She drove her fingers into the thick golden pelt that covered his chest and trailed in a progressively narrowing pattern to his groin. Next, she kneaded his chest, her fingers flexing felinelike, the pads of her fingers testing the resilience of the muscled terrain she discovered.

Micah cupped her breasts. She arched, instincts as old as time making her relish the callused strength of his large hands. Bliss trembled as he plucked her nipples into tight buds.

Starburstlike sensations detonated deep inside her, and she didn't protest when he lifted her up to her knees in front of him. Micah leaned forward, his hands smoothing over her satiny skin as he claimed a turgid nipple and sucked it into his mouth. Shock and pleasure streamed through her veins. She clutched at his shoulders to keep herself from tumbling out of reach.

He sipped at her flesh, tormenting her with feelings so encompassing she could hardly breathe. He moved to her other nipple, tugging at it with careful teeth and laving it with a hot tongue while he closed his hand over the one he'd feasted on just a few moments earlier.

She writhed in his arms and shivered under an onslaught of sensations almost too stimulating to tolerate. "Don't stop," she begged.

He couldn't. He didn't. He held her up, sucking and nipping at her, alternating back and forth from one breast to the other until she felt her body strain and tighten into itself. Bliss reached down, trying to capture his manhood with shaking hands. Micah tumbled her onto her back without warning. She eagerly spread her legs, wanting him inside her and groaning in protest when he simply lodged his powerful loins in the cradle of her parted thighs.

Micah reduced her to a quivering mass with his teeth and tongue, first with his mouth at her breasts, then scattering hot kisses over the satiny skin of her firm belly, and then on to the warm creases that joined her legs to her pelvis. Bracketing her hips with his hands, he held her still and sampled the honeyed heat secreted in the soft, moist folds of her body.

She splintered internally, imploding so violently that she bucked beneath Micah's restraining hands. She felt suspended in the arms of a raging storm as her body shook and her insides spasmed. It seemed to last forever, but she surrendered willingly to the tremors moving through her and the weakness that made her feel boneless. She floated on a cloud of happiness, feeling safe and loved, if only for the moment.

"I'll never get enough of you," Micah muttered, his cheek resting against her thigh as he soothed her with gentle hands.

Bliss smiled and reached down to stroke the side of his face. "I have more to give."

"You're beautiful, Bliss Rowland."

"Don't I wish."

"I can feel your beauty."

"That's good enough for me."

He moved up over her, his powerful arms bracing his weight. "I almost believe you."

"You can, Micah. I wouldn't lie to you. Not ever." *So don't lie to yourself*, she longed to say to him. *Let yourself see with your heart what we can have together.*

He surged into her then, his intrusion hard and thorough. Bliss gasped, then felt her flesh close around him, suck at him, and drench him in the essence of her femininity. She trembled, her desire and her senses revitalized so completely by the throbbing force inside her that she nearly screamed her pleasure. Wrapping her arms and legs around Micah, she returned his passion, driven by the love that blazed like wildfire in her heart and soul.

He thrust deeply, repeatedly, relentlessly, shocking her when he aroused her to a sensually volatile state in a matter of seconds. Her heart raced, and her body clenched and unclenched like a silken fist as Micah pushed the limits of both their bodies. They slammed against each other, almost like adversaries, a passionate craving that seemed vaguely violent spurring them on as they searched together for their own personal summit of pleasure.

Bliss unraveled around him, so suddenly and so completely that she devastated Micah's control.

They drove each other beyond the brink, then tumbled together into the ultimate sensual abyss. The stormy emotions flowing between them colored the joy of their merged bodies and battered hearts with desperation even as they sought and found the pinnacle of a joint release.

She wept his name and her love for him as her climax exploded inside her and sent her orbiting into space.

He hoarsely cried her name as his climax thundered through him, his seed jetting into her steamy depths as he pumped against her.

Clinging to each other, stunned by what had just taken place, they collapsed in a sweaty tangle of limbs in the center of the bed.

Although breathing with great effort, Bliss

refused to censor herself any longer. "I love you, Micah," she gasped.

He gathered her against his heart, too overcome by the impact of her declaration and by the vulnerability he heard in her soft voice to speak at all for several minutes. He held her while she dozed, aware that if he voiced the emotions churning within him, he risked making their parting all the more painful.

He loved her. What man wouldn't? She was the fantasy every man had of a life partner, the one woman capable of fierce loyalty and great compassion. And love. Lord, this talented woman knew how to love, he realized. She gave unstintingly, never holding back, not even when she'd been wounded by a hurtful remark or a cruel attitude.

Micah silently cursed the fate that had sentenced him to a life without vision. His surgeon had warned him that even if his sight was partially restored, he could offer no guarantees. Micah had to live with the constant threat of waking up one morning blind for life, and he refused to subject Bliss to that dark reality.

As she shifted against him, her lips traveling warmly along the side of his neck, he realized that Bliss didn't fully understand his determination not to become dependent on her. He loved her too much, and he refused to use her as a permanent substitute for his lack of vision.

They'd end up hating each other, and he couldn't bear the thought of that happening. He believed in his heart that she deserved much more from the man who loved her, and he had no intention of cheating her of the chance to find a more deserving partner, even if the thought of another man taking her made him physically ill.

"Penny," she whispered as she raised up and peered at him a short while later.

Micah shook his head, the emotions coursing through him thickening his throat and making it difficult to speak. He drew her atop his body, loving the way she curled herself over him until he didn't know where he ended and she began. He wanted her again. Correction, he needed her—and he meant to have her.

"You want me," she whispered, her hands snaking around his neck and her lips so close he could almost taste her.

"Mind reader," he accused.

She laughed. "I won't tell if you won't."

Micah forced himself to focus on the reality they faced, even as she squirmed closer and captured his manhood between her thighs. He gripped her hips, stilling her movement almost instantly.

"What's wrong, Micah?"

You know me too well, he thought, but aloud he said, "Nothing. It's just that there's something I've meant to say to you, and I want to say it now."

"I'm listening."

"You've helped me in more ways than I can ever repay, Bliss, and your efforts haven't been wasted. I won't forget anything you've taught me, nor will I ever forget you."

Something hot splashed on his chest. Other hot tears followed. He realized that he alone had caused her tears, and he loathed himself for complicating her life and causing her pain.

He captured her head with his hands, skimming his thumbs across her damp cheeks. "Don't cry. I want you to remember me with a smile. We've been a hell of a team, haven't we?" He felt her nod before he wrapped his arms around her. "Tell me what you're thinking."

"I believe in you, Micah, and I love you."

The strain he heard in her voice nearly shattered his heart. He took her mouth, all his emotions channeled into the tender joining of their lips and the mating of their tongues. He spoke to her of his love with this single intimacy, rather than with words.

"We have only a few hours left," Bliss reminded him several minutes later. "I don't want to waste them."

"We won't waste a single minute."

They didn't.

Bliss regretted the absence of privacy once they departed Micah's suite shortly before dawn. Cyrus waited for them in the mansion's foyer, carrying his briefcase and looking his usual dapper self.

Bliss knew her father saw the anguish in her eyes, and she felt relieved that he said nothing about it when he hugged her and promised to call her by the end of the day. Micah, wearing sunglasses, a polo shirt, slacks, deck shoes, and the grimmest expression she'd ever seen, took her hand, although he didn't embrace her.

"Be well, Bliss."

"You too."

She stood in the open doorway, numb and disbelieving as she watched them cross the lawn and board the helicopter as the dawn pinkened the sky. Bliss closed the front doors of the mansion before the helicopter lifted off, deliberately, symbolically, cutting herself off from the entire world.

She didn't see or speak to another person for the next week, nor did she cry. She simply had no strength for either endeavor. She dragged herself through the motions of living, eating, bathing, or sleeping when the need arose.

The woman who managed the New York gallery that handled the exhibition and sale of her sculptures finally ended Bliss's self-imposed isolation. Unable to reach her client by phone, she arrived on Saint Thomas, a moving crew in tow.

Bliss stepped back into the world of the living that day. She felt like a candidate for the walking-wounded brigade, flinching at loud sounds and shunning conversations that weren't absolutely necessary. She even resented the brilliant sunshine that bathed the Saint Thomas landscape.

Forced once again to function as a gracious hostess, she grudgingly worked with the moving crew, entertained the gallery owner, and put the finishing touches on the bust of Micah, which she now realized had been properly named "The Heartbreaker." Although she doubted the wisdom of her decision, she reluctantly agreed, after being bullied by the gallery manager, to have the bust displayed with her latest collection, but with the understanding that it wasn't for sale.

Bliss intended to keep the sculpture, if only to remind herself how a man's pride can devastate the dreams of the woman who loves him.

ELEVEN

Flashbulbs winked, champagne corks popped, and the rich and famous chattered, their animated expressions making them look almost like caricatures of themselves. Art critics roamed the sprawling trilevel gallery in Manhattan like hungry predators in search of prey, their inability to conceal their awe at Elizabeth Rowland's latest creative triumph obvious to any onlooker.

A costly array of fragrances scented the air, and the glitter of designer outfits and sparkle of jewels boggled the mind. Limousines continued to pull up to the curb in front of the gallery, spilling additional guests onto the red carpet that led to the front doors of the building before the drivers eased back onto the crowded thoroughfare.

Bliss felt as though she'd been trapped in a room filled with well-heeled, screeching hyenas as the decibel level steadily rose. She escaped the chaos in favor of the landing of a staircase that overlooked the main floor of the gallery, noting with pleasure and a certain amount of shock the Sold signs affixed to nearly all of the pieces in her collection.

She needed a moment apart from the crush of people who'd come to view her sculptures. After two hours spent coping with their questions and effusive praise, Bliss felt exhausted.

She thought about the return flight she'd booked to Saint Thomas for the next morning, relief flooding her at the thought. Bliss desperately wanted to go home. Although she knew she looked composed in her elegant black crepe cocktail sheath, she still felt emotionally fragmented and physically depleted by the stress of the last six weeks.

Her anguish over losing Micah was a constant dull ache that never went away. She took it to bed with her each night, and she woke up with it each morning. It colored her view of the world, casting it into a monochromatic haze. She saw no point in pretending to herself that she didn't need more time to heal. She did.

Cyrus knew the truth, because he'd cared enough to ask. She'd confessed during a particular phone conversation, one of many they'd shared during the previous weeks, that Micah's rejection had hurt her as deeply as the loss of her mother. Although Cyrus admitted that he couldn't offer her a solution, he'd listened with paternal love. He counseled patience, with herself and with Micah. She trusted that he had her best interests at heart, and she tried to follow his advice.

Bliss spotted Cyrus and his security guards as they stepped into the gallery. She smiled, delighted that he'd finally arrived. It was the first opening night he'd ever attended, although his invitations had always been messenger-delivered by the gallery manager. She watched the security detail clear a path through the crowd, and she met her father at the foot of the staircase.

After a warm embrace, he drew her off to the side, his arm sliding around her shoulders as they stepped into an alcove that provided a modicum of privacy. "You look splendid, but still a little pale."

"I'll be fine, Dad. The last few weeks have been a circus, but I'm going home in the morning."

"To start another collection, or to get some rest?"

"A little bit of both, I hope, even though I haven't even thought about what I'll do next. I feel as though my life's suspended in limbo at the moment."

He glanced past her, his eyes widening when someone or something across the room caught his attention. Bliss followed his gaze. Her smile slipped, then disappeared altogether. She paled even more.

She stared at Micah, who stood in front of one of her more erotic sculptures. She couldn't tear her eyes from him. Clad in a dark suit that shouted the name of a European men's clothier, a crisp white shirt, and silk tie, he looked composed and elegant. He could also see, she realized, shock roaring through her like a tornado. He wore gold-rimmed aviator-style glasses, which gave him an arrogantly sexy look that reminded Bliss of Robert Redford in his prime. Swaying suddenly, she felt torn between her happiness for Micah that his vision had been restored and her anger with herself for allowing him to put her through such hell.

Cyrus frowned at her and gripped her upper arms. Moving sideways, he deliberately blocked her view of Micah. "Steady, young lady."

She blinked and peered at her father. She thought he looked guilty, and she immediately knew why.

"Micah's still doing battle with his pride, so

try to be patient enough to let him come to you when he's ready."

Her voice faint, she asked, "Did you invite him?"

"Would you object if I had?"

"I'm not sure." She exhaled softly, determined to regain control of herself. "I didn't send him an invitation. Before you say one word, you should know that I have no intention of begging the man to pay attention to me."

"Begging's not your style, Bliss. It never will be, and I certainly wouldn't suggest that you acquire the skill. You're a proud woman, just as Micah's a proud man."

"His pride's like an albatross around his neck," she muttered. "At least I use mine to keep my standards high."

"Pride can make you stiff-necked and inaccessible. Take it from an expert. Perhaps you should think of your time together at the estate as water under the proverbial dam. You can't change what's happened, but you can start fresh."

"There's nothing I did that I want to change. I don't regret the time I spent with Micah. What I resent is the way he ended things between us."

A waiter stepped into the alcove, a collection of filled champagne goblets on his tray. Cyrus took one for himself, but Bliss shook her head, her eyes darting back to Micah once again.

"He looks stronger and more confident now, doesn't he?" she said softly a few moments later.

Cyrus nodded. "But he's been through hell, Bliss."

She returned her attention to her father. "I don't even know what to say to him if he comes up to me. I'm torn between punching him and hugging him."

Cyrus chuckled. "Your mother punched me once. I think it happened on our honeymoon. Knocked me clear into the next week."

"Mother hit you?" Bliss couldn't hide her disbelief. When her father flushed, she laughed in amazement.

"It wasn't a fight. We were fooling around. Let's just say I got in the way of her hand and leave it at that."

"I'm glad you have good memories of Mom."

"You'd be amazed by how many good memories I do have." He sobered. "As for the situation with Micah, why don't you just listen to what he has to say?"

"He may not even speak to me."

Cyrus raised a bushy eyebrow and scowled at her.

"All right, I'll listen," she promised, then

defiantly added, "but I'm not promising anything more."

He linked their arms. "How about a guided tour of your collection? From the look of this crowd you obviously have another success on your hands."

Bliss smiled, grateful for the change of subject. "I'm glad you're here to share it with me."

On the opposite side of the gallery Micah moved from sculpture to sculpture, his respect and admiration for Bliss's artistry growing with every sculpture he viewed. He maintained a discreet distance from Cyrus and Bliss, but he kept them in sight as he skirted the clusters of people milling about in the gallery.

He felt mired in guilt and regret, especially after seeing the shocked dismay in her expression when she'd first spotted him in the crowd. He reminded himself that he was here because he owed her the truth, not just because he loved her. He wondered, though, if she still cared enough about him to listen to what he needed to say to her.

Wandering down a congested corridor nearly an hour later, Micah paused at the entrance to a high-ceilinged room that housed additional works by other artists. He noticed the life-size bust as soon as he stepped into the room, his heart speeding up to a double-time march in his chest. Slowly approaching the pedestal that held the sculpture, he glanced down at the brass placque that read: "HEART-BREAKER." BLISS ROWLAND. DISPLAY ONLY.

Stunned, Micah stared at the sculpted clay rendering of his chest and head. He saw a new element of her talent in the realism that had influenced her approach to the work, as well as her scrupulous attention to detail and extraordinary memory, for she'd seen his eyes as a seventeen-year-old girl. He saw the love she'd put into her perception of him, and he realized how greatly he'd failed her.

But most of all, he glimpsed himself through the eyes of a gifted woman who'd said she loved him and believed in him at a time when he hadn't cared enough to believe in himself. Here was the proof of her love. She'd allowed the art world to see it, but he wondered if she'd intended for him to view it as well. Remorse flooded him, momentarily paralyzing him with regret until he regained control over his emotions.

Micah couldn't walk away from the bust, so he indulged himself and studied it at length. He tried to imagine his future without Bliss. The bleakness of it made him wince. Unwittingly she strengthened his sense of purpose as he stood and stared at his own image, and she inspired him with renewed hope that she might speak with him before she left New York.

He found her with Cyrus and a small group of her father's cronies from the diplomatic community. He paused a few feet from where she stood, but he waited for her to decide whether or not to greet him. A ragged sigh escaped him when she finally excused herself and approached him.

"Hello, Micah. Congratulations on the obvious success of your surgery. I'm happy for you."

He nodded, unwilling to tell her the details or the realities just yet. Her rigid posture and composed manner worried him, but it didn't distract him from reacting to her appearance. "I didn't expect you to be so beautiful."

She smiled coolly. "What's that old adage about 'the eye of the beholder'?" she asked as she looked up at him.

"The package matches the contents, Bliss. I spent enough time around you to know what you're made of."

"Perhaps."

"We both know I did," he declared, so hungry for her that he wanted to take her into his arms and carry her off to a private retreat as far away from the rest of the world as possible.

She flinched, but she didn't back away. Micah stared at her, his gaze hot and possessive. He couldn't forget the satiny feel of her skin. The memory of touching her, making love with her, had kept him awake night after agonizing night during their weeks apart. He wanted to touch her again, *needed* to touch her again, but he closed his hands into fists instead. His instincts told him that she would reject his touch.

He knew he had no rights over her any longer. He'd abandoned them, all in the name of masculine pride. He watched her tongue dart out to moisten her lips, and he suddenly remembered her taste. His senses stirred, and the muscles in his large frame tensed as he swallowed his need. How, he wondered, could he have been so stupid as to walk out on this remarkable woman?

She quickly filled the silence that stretched between them. "I hope you enjoyed the sculptures."

Alarm lanced through him. He sensed her desire to dismiss him after a few minutes of polite conversation. "Can we get together before you leave New York?" Micah asked.

Bliss stiffened. "I'm leaving in the morning."

"How about tonight? We need to talk."

"I'm at the Plaza. Why don't you call me later? I still have to pack, so I'll be up quite late."

"I'd hoped we could go somewhere for a late supper."

"I'm not hungry, Micah."

"A glass of wine, then. I know a place near here that I think you'd enjoy."

She shook her head. "Why don't you phone me at the hotel? I'll let the operator know it's all right to put your call through, regardless of the time." Bliss backed up a step. "My guests are waiting, so I'll say good night now."

He watched her start to turn away, but he moved quickly and blocked her path without touching her. He felt ostracized and unimportant, and resentment flared to life inside him. "Bliss, I've been a complete fool—"

Her chin rose. The green in her eyes darkened. "You and me both," she said in a tight, tense, dismissive voice. Head held high, she stepped around him and rejoined Cyrus, who frowned in Micah's direction.

Hands fisted at his sides, Micah turned on his heel and strode out of the gallery. He climbed into the first cab that slid up to the curb and glared at the driver until the man asked for his destination. "The Plaza," he barked, the fury he felt engulfing him.

Thirty minutes later he watched Bliss walk into the lobby of the Plaza Hotel. Alone. He followed her to the elevator, noting how preoccupied she seemed. He paused a few feet behind her and waited for her to glance his way. She did almost immediately. He watched the shock that widened her eyes and leached the color from her cheeks through narrowed, wary eyes.

The elevator doors opened. Micah stepped inside after her, settling against the back wall of the conveyance while Bliss edged to a position near the side wall. He ignored her glare, and he excused her silence. Her palpable anger prompted him to ponder the change in her attitude. He'd cornered her, and, he realized, she resented him.

His gaze fell to the pulse that throbbed in the hollow of her throat. He noticed, too, that Bliss grew progressively more pale as the elevator ascended to the penthouse level.

The doors opened, and Micah caught her wrist as she started to exit the elevator. "Are you all right?"

She tugged free of his hold and absently rubbed her wrist. She saw his concern in the rich blue of his eyes, but she didn't indulge herself with the idea that he really cared how she felt. "I'm fine, but thank you for asking."

"Cut it out, Bliss."

"Cut what out?" she demanded.

"This demonstration of good manners."

She lifted her chin in defiance and swept past him. When she realized that Micah wasn't behind her, she paused and looked over her shoulder. "Are you joining me or not?"

He nodded curtly and made his way down the hall at her side. She unlocked the door, the agitated state of her nerves making her hand shake as she inserted the key and turned the knob. He followed her inside, securing the lock while she shrugged free of her cape and dropped it and her purse on the first chair she passed. She came to a halt when she ran out of floor space. Facing him from the opposite side of the room, her arms crossed beneath her breasts, her legs slightly parted in a stance that spoke eloquently of her determination not to be bullied by him, she kept her facial expression blank.

Bliss watched Micah shed his jacket, then loosen his tie and jerk it off before releasing the top three buttons of his shirt. He didn't bother to sit down. He prowled, aimlessly, restlessly, around the sitting room. She knew he wasn't even registering the Old World elegance of the penthouse suite.

"Cyrus thought I should listen to what you have to say."

Micah stopped abruptly. "Whether or not you wanted to?"

She ignored his sarcasm. "I'm listening, Micah."

"You're suspicious of me, aren't you?"

She heard the shock in his voice, but she refused to let it move her. He had the ability to wound her again, and she resisted the notion of giving him that kind of power.

"I don't understand your motive for being here," she admitted.

"This isn't easy, Bliss. I'm not even sure where to start."

Her gaze traveled to the bar. "Would you like a drink?"

Micah swore, the word so lethal that she backed up a step. She felt the press of a chair cushion against the back of her legs, and gratefully sank down onto it.

"I've never seen this side of you before," he observed.

"Self-protective? Wary?" she asked, her voice controlled as she studied him. "Furious with your high-handed behavior?"

He nodded. "You're wearing one hell of a suit of armor."

She frowned at him, then reverted to her gracious-hostess routine. "Did you want a drink, Micah? There's a nice cognac in the bar."

"I don't want a damn drink!" he shouted. "Quit pretending to be Emily Post. You're driving me crazy. You're talking to the man who knows every intimate detail of your body, not some fool who just fell off the turnip truck."

She balked at his loss of temper and his reference to the intimate acts they'd shared. "Don't swear at me, and don't yell at me either. You don't have the right to treat me this way."

He squared his shoulders, his blue eyes blazing with emotions she didn't understand as he glared at her from his position in the center of the spacious sitting room. "You're a strong woman, the kind of woman I've always wanted in my life."

She relented a little, but then she reminded herself that he hadn't said she was *the* woman he wanted in his life. She longed to say, "I don't feel strong, Micah. I feel wounded and vulnerable, and I'm frightened about the power you have over me because I love you." But she didn't. Instead, she admitted, "I feel like I'm in pieces and scattered all over the landscape."

He unclenched his fists, making an obvious effort to calm down. "I always knew you were a beautiful person, but I had no real grasp on how lovely you really are."

She felt knocked off balance by his change in tactics. "Nice clothes and an effective use of cosmetics. In short, a public image that has little to do with the person beneath the fabric and the paint," she said with a dismissive shrug.

"Since my appearance isn't why you're here, there's no reason to dwell on it."

"I'm ashamed of the way I've behaved."

Bliss stared. She couldn't help herself. She believed him. She couldn't not believe him. The distress etched into his hard features and the tension vibrating through his large body confirmed that Micah spoke the truth. Still, she grappled silently with her amazement, and she didn't completely let down her guard.

He raked a hand through his thick golden hair. "This is awkward, Bliss."

"I agree."

Unable to stop herself, she let her gaze dip beneath his chin; it lingered briefly at his strong throat and snagged on the chest hair visible in the unbuttoned V of his crisp white shirt. He'd lost some of his tan during their weeks apart, but she thought he still looked wonderful. She pressed her palms together, aware that she wanted nothing more than to slip into his arms and rediscover the warmth and vitality of his muscular body for herself.

"You still look tense."

She stiffened, her green eyes widening. "What makes you believe that how I look or feel or think concerns you?"

"It should," he declared. "Hell, it does."

She frowned. "Why? You rejected me, and

you didn't look back. I am not now, nor have I ever been, your responsibility."

"When a man cares about a woman, he wants the best for her. I want what's best for you. I always have. I thought giving you your freedom was the right thing to do. I didn't want you to wake up one morning regretting our relationship. I still don't."

"Really?" She didn't try to hide her disbelief. "So you just walked out on me instead. You didn't bother to ask me what I wanted, because you assumed you knew what was best for me. Micah Holbrook, you think twice before you ever do what's best for me again. I'm not some little airhead with a short attention span. I'm an adult with values and standards and principles. Is all that garbled thinking of yours the reason you decided to make decisions about my happiness for me? Is that why you let your ego and your damnable pride stand in the way of your own happiness?"

He nodded with obvious reluctance, then tried to defend himself. "My ego was badly dented, and my pride kept me from telling you how much I appreciated you. It took me a while to understand that my ability to see was never the real issue."

"What was the issue?" she asked. She prayed that he'd come to terms with his self-doubt, because she knew she'd never survive it if he lulled her into thinking they had a chance for a relationship and then walked out on her again.

"If I hadn't let my ego get in the way, I would have understood far sooner the value of caring for a woman and being cared for by her in return."

Bliss couldn't sit still any longer. She vibrated with anxiety about what he might *not* say. Abandoning her chair, she crossed the room and paused at the bar. She filled a crystal tumbler with ice and poured Perrier over the cubes. When Micah's hands settled on her shoulders, she jerked in surprise. Her drink slipped out of her hand before she could stop it, the crystal shattering in the bottom of the bar's sink.

He forced her to turn around, then held her still with his hands at her waist. "Talk to me. Tell me how you feel."

"Please don't touch me," she whispered, her insides quivering with response to the feel of his hands on her. "It hurts too much to remember that part. I don't . . ." She blinked back the tears that filled her eyes. "I don't want to remember."

"You really don't want to remember how good we were together?" he asked hoarsely.

Bliss bowed her head and pressed her fingertips to her temples. She felt his arms slide around her waist. She rested her forehead against his chest, but just for a moment. "That's all I ever seem to do."

"You're not the only one. I think about you constantly. I can't get you out of my mind."

She ducked beneath his hands and made her way to a window that provided an extraordinary view of the city at night. Micah followed her, but he didn't attempt to touch her again. He stood beside her, his hands jammed into his pants pockets as he stared at the twinkling lights that stretched for endless miles in front of them.

"I'm seeing the world differently now," he said. "I've never had anyone fight for me the way you did. It was a humbling experience to realize that I needed anybody so much. I couldn't accept the idea of being dependent on you, because I've never known how to depend on anyone but myself. I'm not even certain I can learn and not feel compromised by the process."

Bliss felt her control slip and her anxiety return full force. She understood him now, she realized. He was trying to let her down gently, and she was giving him the fight of his life, but he persisted, trying to make his point with words like "caring," "appreciation," and "dependence."

She felt like an idiot. Exhaling softly, she

wanted to change the adversarial tone of their conversation, wanted to make peace with him once and for all, because she couldn't hate him. She loved Micah too much to reduce her feelings for him to a pile of ashes. She also loved him enough to do what was best for him, and that meant letting go and wishing him well.

Bliss turned and faced him, willing now to forgive and forget. He obviously couldn't love her the way she needed to be loved, and she hoped she could find a way to accept an uncomplicated friendship.

"Micah, there's no need to subject yourself to this confession. Perhaps there'll come a time when we can reclaim the friendship that started our relationship. I hope so, but this isn't the time. It's too soon for me. I still hurt too much. I want you in ways that clearly aren't right for you, and I understand that now. Why don't we both give ourselves some time to come to terms with what we shared? We can keep in touch through Cyrus."

His stricken look baffled her. She already felt on the verge of sobbing, and the last thing she wanted was to embarrass either one of them. "It's late."

"I was a fool to think you'd even consider taking me back, wasn't I?"

She stared at him, stunned, certain she'd misunderstood him. "What did you say?"

"You heard me, Bliss. I love you, but I didn't want to be a burden, a burden you might learn to hate."

"You were never a burden!" she exclaimed, still not quite able to believe her ears. "Not ever, do you understand? I love you, Micah. Didn't you believe me when I told you how I felt about you?"

"I wanted to, but I was sure you'd change your mind and decide that what you actually felt for me was empathy, not love."

"I wish I'd realized how torn you were. I was so busy trying to keep my feelings separate from the reason Cyrus sent you to me in the first place, I guess I wasn't thinking clearly half the time either."

Micah pulled her into his arms and held her so tightly that he nearly crushed her ribs. He found her mouth, plundering it with a thoroughness that weakened her knees and sent her pulse into overdrive. She felt the need that sent shudders through his body and a surge of hard power into his loins. Bliss molded herself to him, loving the feel and the promise of his arousal until he abruptly separated their bodies, his breathing harsh as he struggled for control.

Dazed, Bliss steadied herself and stared up at him. Lifting her hands, she smoothed her thumbs over his dense brows as she drove her fingers into her short hair. "I believe in you, Micah. And I love—"

He shook his head. "There's something you don't know yet, and you need to hear it before you say anything more."

She sobered when she saw his serious expression and put the brakes on her relief that he loved her. Something obviously still troubled him, but she felt determined to work through any reservations he had. Bliss managed a reassuring smile and suggested, "Why don't we sit down?"

They walked over to the couch. Micah pulled her into his lap after sitting down. Removing his glasses, he massaged the bridge of his nose. Bliss decided he was gathering his thoughts, and she found the patience to let him speak in his own good time, despite her concern about what he might say.

"My vision is only partially restored, and the doctors feel certain it will fail again. Probably within five years. Unless some pretty revolutionary technology comes down the pike between now and then, I will be permanently blind." He replaced his glasses and met her gaze. "Can you live with that? Can you really spend your life with a man incapable of seeing the results of your creative endeavors or the faces of our children as they grow up?"

She looked into his eyes unflinchingly and

replied, "It makes me sad for you, but it doesn't frighten me. I fell in love with Micah Holbrook, the whole man. I will love you under any and all circumstances. As long as we're together, I'll be happy." Bliss slipped her arms around his neck. "With luck you'll see our babies, but it won't matter to them as they grow up whether or not their father can see. What will matter is if you love them."

"You're sure? Once I have you, I won't let you go."

"Would you leave me if I had an accident and lost the use of my legs?"

"Of course not. I love you, Bliss, more than my life."

"Then we're both willing to take the same risks. Micah, I can't remember a time since I was seventeen years old that I didn't love you, but now I love you with the passion and maturity that makes a commitment possible. Did you honestly think I'd have reservations about us because of your vision, after all we've been through together?"

He had the good sense to look chagrined."I hoped you wouldn't, but I wanted you to be certain, for both our sakes."

"My only concern is that you trust me to know what I want, because I want you, whether your eyes have sight or not. There's an upside to this. You'll have more time to prepare yourself." She smiled. "Since you didn't protest the possibility of having babies, is it safe to assume we're getting married?"

He laughed for the first time all evening. "Makes sense to me. Oh, I should warn you. Cyrus wants me on board as a security consultant once the navy cuts me loose." Micah stood, keeping her cradled against his chest. "Where's the bedroom in this place?"

Bliss grinned and pointed at an open doorway. "Are we starting on the babies already?"

"Not this time, but soon." He nuzzled the side of her neck. "We have to call Cyrus first, anyway."

Miffed, she reminded him, "His permission isn't required. I thought I already explained that to you weeks ago."

He dropped a hard kiss on her parted lips. "I need to know when he's available to escort you down the aisle."

"I'll make sure he's free on Saturday," Bliss promised as Micah crossed the bedroom, tossed off an oblique comment about too many antiques, and made a beeline for the bed.

Seconds later, she stood naked atop the mattress, Micah's fingertips skimming the surface of her sensitive skin. "You're still dressed," she pointed out breathlessly, her breasts firming and her nipples tightening to dagger points beneath his busy fingers.

Micah gave her a wry look as she dropped to her knees in the middle of the bed and dragged the covers out of the way. He shed his clothes without any further urging. As Bliss watched the remarkable flex and flow of his muscled frame, she thought about the sculpture she intended to do of her future husband. It would be a nude and confined to their private collection, because she had no intention of sharing him with the world.

"Heartbreaker" would remain a part of their collection, of course, but only as a symbol of her love for Micah.

He joined her then, pulling her into his arms and telling her as he tugged her down and tucked her beneath him about all the ways he intended to love her for the rest of their lives.

THE EDITOR'S CORNER

The heroines in September's LOVESWEPT novels have a secret dream of love and passion—and they find the answer to their wishes with FANTASY MEN! Whether he's a dangerous rogue, a dashing prince, or a lord of the jungle, he's a masterful hero who knows just the right moves that dazzle the senses, the teasing words that stoke white-hot desire, and the seductive caresses that promise ecstasy. He's the kind of man who can make a woman do anything, the only man who can fulfill her deepest longing. And the heroines find they'll risk all, even their hearts, to make their dreams come true with FANTASY MEN. . . .

Our first dream lover sizzles off the pages of Sandra Chastain's **THE MORNING AFTER**, LOVESWEPT #636. Razor Cody had come to Savannah seeking revenge on the man who'd destroyed his business, but instead he found a fairy-tale princess whose violet eyes and spun-gold hair made him yearn for what he'd never dared to hope would be his! Rachel Kimble told him she'd known he was coming and hinted of the treasure he'd find if he stayed, but she couldn't conceal her shocking desire for the mysterious stranger! Vowing to keep her safe from shadows that haunted her nights, Razor fought to heal Rachel's pain, as her gentle touch soothed his own. **THE MORNING AFTER** is Sandra Chastain at her finest.

Cindy Gerard invites you to take one last summer swim with her fantasy man in **DREAM TIDE**, LOVESWEPT #637. Patrick Ryan was heart-stoppingly gorgeous—all temptation and trouble in a pair of jeans. And Merry Clare Thomas was stunned to wake up in his arms . . . and in his bed! She'd taken refuge in her rental cottage, never expecting the tenant to return that night—or that he'd look exactly like the handsome wanderer of a hundred years ago who'd been making steamy love to her in her dreams every night for a week. Was it destiny or just coincidence that Pat called her his flame, his firebrand, just as her dream lover had? Overwhelmed by need, dazzled by passion, Merry responded with fierce pleasure to Pat's wildfire caresses, possessed by him in a magical enchantment that just couldn't be real. But Cindy's special touch is all too real in this tale of a fantasy come true.

TROUBLE IN PARADISE, LOVESWEPT #638, is another winner from one of LOVESWEPT's rising stars, Susan Connell. Just lying in a hammock, Reilly Anderson awakened desire potent enough to take her breath away, but Allison Richards fought her attraction to the bare-chested hunk who looked like he'd stepped out of an adventure movie! Gazing at the long-legged vision who insisted that he help her locate her missing brother-in-law, Reilly knew that trouble had arrived . . . the kind of trouble a man just had to taste! Reilly drew her into a paradise of pleasure, freeing her spirit with tender savagery and becoming her very own Tarzan, Lord of the Jungle. He swore he'd make her see she had filled his heart with joy and that he'd never let her go.

Linda Jenkins's fantasy is a **SECRET ADMIRER**, LOVESWEPT #639. An irresistible rascal, Jack was the golden prince of her secret girlhood fantasies, but Kary Lucas knew Jack Rowland could never be hers! Back then he'd always teased her about being the smartest girl in town—how could she believe the charming nomad with the bad-boy grin when he insisted he was home to stay at last? Jack infuriated her and made her ache with sensual longing. But when mysterious gifts began arriving, presents and notes that seemed to know her private passions, Kary was torn: tempted by the romance of her unknown knight, yet thrilled by the explosive heat of Jack's embraces, the insatiable need he aroused. Linda's fantasy man has just the right combination of dreamy mystery and thrilling reality to keep your nights on fire!

Terry Lawrence works her own unique LOVESWEPT magic with **DANCING ON THE EDGE**, LOVESWEPT #640. Stunt coordinator Greg Ford needed a woman to stand up to him, to shake him up, and Annie Oakley Cartwright decided she was just the brazen daredevil to do it! Something burned between them from the moment they met, made Annie want to rise to his challenge, to tempt the man who made her lips tingle just by looking. Annie trusted him with her body, ached to ease his sorrow with her rebel's heart. Once she'd reminded him life was a series of gambles, and love the biggest one of all, she could only hope he would dance with his spitfire as long as their music played. Terry's spectacular romance will send you looking for your own stuntman!

Leanne Banks has a regal fantasy man for you in **HIS ROYAL PLEASURE**, LOVESWEPT #641. Prince Alex swept into her peaceful life like a swashbuckling pirate, confidently expecting Katherine Kendall to let him spend a month at her island camp—never confessing the secret of his birth to the sweet and tender lady who made him want to break all the rules! He made her feel beautiful, made her dream of dancing in the dark and succumbing to forbidden kisses under a moonlit sky. Katherine wondered who he was, but Alex was an expert when it came to games lovers play, and he made her moan with ecstasy at his sizzling touch . . . until she learned his shocking secret. Leanne is at her steamy best with this sexy fantasy man.

Happy reading!

With warmest wishes,

Nita Taublib

Associate Publisher

P.S. On the next pages is a preview of the Bantam titles on sale *now* at your favorite bookstore.

Don't miss these exciting books by your favorite Bantam authors

On sale in July:
FANTA C
by Sandra Brown

CRY WOLF
by Tami Hoag

TWICE IN A LIFETIME
by Christy Cohen

THE TESTIMONY
by Sharon and Tom Curtis

And in hardcover from Doubleday
STRANGER IN MY ARMS
by R. J. Kaiser

From *New York Times*
Bestselling Author

Sandra Brown

Fanta C

The bestselling author of Temperatures Rising *and*
French Silk, *Sandra Brown has created a sensation with her*
contemporary novels. Now, in this classic novel she offers a
tender, funny, and deeply sensual story about a woman
caught between the needs of her children, her career, and her
own passionate heart.

Elizabeth Burke's days are filled with the business of
running an elegant boutique and caring for her two
small children. But her nights are long and empty
since the death of her husband two years before,
and she spends them dreaming of the love and romance
that might have been. Then Thad Randolph steps
into her life—a man right out of her most intimate
fantasies.

Elizabeth doesn't believe in fairy tales, and she knows
all too well that happy endings happen only in books.
Now she wishes she could convince herself that friend-

ship is all she wants from Thad. But the day will come when she'll finally have to make a choice—to remain forever true to her memories or to let go of the past and risk loving once more.

Cry Wolf
by
Tami Hoag

author of *Still Waters* and *Lucky's Lady*

Tami Hoag is one of today's premier writers of romantic suspense. Publisher's Weekly *calls her "a master of the genre" for her powerful combination of gripping suspense and sizzling passion. Now from the incredibly talented author of Sarah's Sin, Lucky's Lady, and Still Waters comes Cry Wolf, her most dangerously thrilling novel yet. . . .*

All attorney Laurel Chandler wanted was a place to hide, to escape the painful memories of a case that had destroyed her career, her marriage, and nearly her life. But coming home to the peaceful, tree-lined streets of her old hometown won't give Laurel the serenity she craves. For in the sultry heat of a Louisiana summer, she'll find herself pursued by Jack Boudreaux, a gorgeous stranger whose carefree smile hides a private torment . . . and by a murderer who enjoys the hunt as much as the kill.

In the following scene, Laurel is outside of Frenchie's, a local hangout, when she realizes she's unable to drive the car she borrowed. When Jack offers to drive her home, she has no alternative but to accept.

"Women shouldn't accept rides from men they barely know," she said, easing herself down in the bucket seat, her gaze fixed on Jack.

"What?" he asked, splaying a hand across his bare chest, the picture of hurt innocence. "You think *I'm* the Bayou Strangler? Oh, man . . ."

"You could be the man."

"What makes you think it's a man? Could be a woman."

"Could be, but not likely. Serial killers tend to be white males in their thirties."

He grinned wickedly, eyes dancing. "Well, I fit that bill, I guess, but I don't have to kill ladies to get what I want, angel."

He leaned into her space, one hand sliding across the back of her seat, the other edging along the dash, corralling her. Laurel's heart kicked into overdrive as he came closer, though fear was not the dominant emotion. It should have been, but it wasn't.

That strange sense of desire and anticipation crept along her nerves. If she leaned forward, he would kiss her. She could see the promise in his eyes and felt something wild and reckless and completely foreign to her rise up in answer, pushing her to close the distance, to take the chance. His eyes dared her, his mouth lured—masculine, sexy, lips slightly parted in invitation. What fear she felt was of herself, of this attraction she didn't want.

"It's power, not passion," she whispered, barely able to find her voice at all.

Jack blinked. The spell was broken. "What?"

"They kill for power. Exerting power over other human beings gives them a sense of omnipotence . . . among other things."

He sat back and fired the 'Vette's engine, his brows drawn as he contemplated what she'd said. "So, why are you going with me?"

"Because there are a dozen witnesses standing on the gallery who saw me get in the car with you. You'd be the last person seen with me alive, which would automatically make you a suspect. Patrons in the bar will testify that I spurned your advances. That's motive. If you were the killer, you'd be pretty stupid to take me away from here and kill me, and if this killer was stupid, someone would have caught him by now."

He scowled as he put the car in gear. "And here I thought you'd say it was my charm and good looks."

"Charming men don't impress me," she said flatly, buckling her seat belt.

Then what does? Jack wondered as he guided the car slowly out of the parking lot. A sharp mind, a man of principles? He had one, but wasn't the other. Not that it mattered. He wasn't interested in Laurel Chandler. She would be too much trouble. And she was too uptight to go for a man who spent most of his waking hours at Frenchie's—unlike her sister, who went for any man who could get it up. Night and day, those two. He couldn't help wondering why.

The Chandler sisters had been raised to be belles. Too good for the likes of him, ol' Blackie would have said. Too good for a no-good coonass piece of trash. He glanced across at Laurel, who sat with her hands folded and her glasses perched on her slim little nose and thought the old man would have been right. She was prim and proper, Miss Law and Order, full of morals and high ideals and upstanding qualities . . . and fire . . . and pain . . . and secrets in her eyes. . . .

"Was I to gather from that conversation with T-Grace that you used to be an attorney?" she asked as they turned onto Dumas and headed back toward downtown.

He smiled, though it held no real amusement, only cynicism. "Sugar, 'attorney' is too polite a word for what I used to be. I was a corporate shark for Tristar Chemical."

Laurel tried to reconcile the traditional three-piece-suit corporate image with the man who sat across from her, a baseball cap jammed down backward on his head, his Hawaiian shirt hanging open to reveal the hard, tanned body of a light heavyweight boxer. "What happened?"

What happened? A simple question as loaded as a shotgun that had been primed and pumped. What happened? He had succeeded. He had set out to prove to his old man that he could do something, be something, make big money. It hadn't mattered that Blackie was long dead and gone to hell.

The old man's ghost had driven him. He had succeeded, and in the end he had lost everything.

"I turned on 'em," he said, skipping the heart of the story. The pain he endured still on Evie's behalf was his own private hell. He didn't share it with anyone. "*Rogue Lawyer*. I think they're gonna make it into a TV movie one of these days."

"What do you mean, you turned on them?"

"I mean, I unraveled the knots I'd tied for them in the paper trail that divorced them from the highly illegal activities of shipping and dumping hazardous waste," he explained, not entirely sure why he was telling her. Most of the time when people asked, he just blew it off, made a joke, and changed the subject. "The Feds took a dim view of the company. The company gave me the ax, and the Bar Association kicked my ass out."

"You were disbarred for revealing illegal, potentially dangerous activities to the federal government?" Laurel said, incredulous. "But that's—"

"The way it is, sweetheart," he growled, slowing the 'Vette as the one and only stop light in Bayou Breaux turned red. He rested his hand on the stick shift and gave Laurel a hard look. "Don' make me out to be a hero, sugar. I'm nobody's saint. I lost it," he said bitterly. "I crashed and burned. I went down in a ball of flame, and I took the company with me. I had my reasons, and none of them had anything to do with such noble causes as the protection of the environment."

"But—"

" 'But,' you're thinking now, 'mebbe this Jack, he isn't such a bad guy after all,' yes?" His look turned sly, speculative. He chuckled as she frowned. She didn't want to think he could read her so easily. If they'd been playing poker, he would have cleaned out her pockets.

"Well, you're wrong, angel," he murmured darkly, his mouth twisting with bitter amusement as her blue eyes widened. "I'm as bad as they come." Then he flashed his famous grin, dimples biting into his cheeks. "But I'm a helluva good time."

Twice in a Lifetime
by
Christy Cohen

author of *Private Scandals*

Fifteen years ago, an act of betrayal tore four best friends apart . . .

SARAH. *A lonely newlywed in a new town, she was thrilled when Annabel came into her life. Suddenly Sarah had someone to talk to and the best part was that her husband seemed to like Annabel too.*
JESSE. *With his sexy good looks and dangerous aura, he could have had any woman. But he'd chosen sweet, innocent Sarah, who touched not only his body but his soul. So why couldn't Jesse stop dreaming of his wife's best friend?*
ANNABEL. *Beautiful, desirable, and enigmatic, she yearned for something more exciting than being a wife and mother. And nothing was more exciting than making a man like Jesse want her.*
PATRICK. *Strong and tender, this brilliant scientist learned that the only way to keep Annabel his wife was to turn a blind eye—until the day came when he couldn't pretend anymore.*

In the following scene, Jesse and Annabel feel trapped at a birthday party that Sarah is hosting and they have to escape into the surrounding neighborhood.

As they walked through the neighborhood of newer homes, Jesse's arm was around her. He could feel every curve of her. Her breast was pressed against his chest. Her leg brushed his as she walked.

"Sarah's probably pissed," he said.

Annabel laughed. "She'll get over it. Besides, Patrick the knight will save her."

Jesse looked at her.

"Have you noticed they've been talking to each other a lot?"

"Of course. Patrick calls her from work. And sometimes at night. He's too honest not to tell me."

When Annabel pressed herself closer to Jesse, he lowered his hand a little on her shoulder. An inch or two farther down and he would be able to touch the silky skin of her breast.

"Do you love him?" he asked.

Annabel stopped suddenly and Jesse dropped his hand. She turned to stare at him.

"What do you think?"

With her eyes challenging him, Jesse took a step closer.

"I think you don't give a fuck about him. Maybe you did when you married him, but it didn't last long. Now it's me you're after."

Annabel tossed back her black hair, laughing.

"God, what an ego. You think a little harmless flirting means I'm hot for you. No wonder Sarah needed a change of pace."

Jesse grabbed her face in one hand and squeezed. He watched tears come to her eyes as he increased the pressure on her jaw, but she didn't cry out.

"Sarah did not cheat on me," he said. "You got the story wrong."

He pushed her away and started walking back toward the house. Annabel took a deep breath, then came after him.

"What Sarah did or didn't do isn't the point," she said when she reached him. "She's not the one who's unhappy."

Jesse glanced at her, but kept walking.

"You're saying I am?"

"It's obvious, Jesse. Little Miss Perfect Sarah isn't all that exciting. Especially for a man like you. I'll bet that's why you have to ride your Harley all the time. To replace all the passion you gave up when you married her."

Jesse looked up over the houses, to Mt. Rainier in the distance.

"I sold the bike," he said. "Two weeks ago."

"My God, why?"

Jesse stopped again.

"Because Sarah asked me to. And because, no matter what you think, I love her."

They stared at each other for a long time. The wind was cool and Jesse watched gooseflesh prickle Annabel's skin. He didn't know whom he was trying to convince more, Annabel or himself.

"I think we should go back," Jesse said.

Annabel nodded. "Of course. You certainly don't want to make little Sarah mad. You've got to be the dutiful husband. If Sarah says sell your bike, you sell your bike. If she wants you to entertain twelve kids like a clown, then you do it. If—"

Jesse grabbed her, only intending to shut her up. But when he looked down at her, he knew she had won. She had been whittling away at him from the very beginning. She had made him doubt himself, and Sarah, and everything he thought he should be. He grabbed her hair and tilted her head back. She slid her hands up around his neck. Her fingers were cool and silky.

Later, he would look back and try to convince himself that she was the one who initiated the kiss, that she pulled his head down and pressed her red lips to his. Maybe she initiated it, maybe he did. All he knew was that he was finally touching her, kissing her, his tongue was in her mouth and it felt better than he'd ever imagined.

The Testimony

A classic romance by

Sharon & Tom Curtis

bestselling authors of *The Golden Touch*

*It had been so easy falling in love with Jesse Ludan . . .
with his ready smile and laughing green eyes, his sensual
body and clever journalist's mind. The day Christine became
his wife was the happiest day of her life. But for the past six
months, Jesse's idealism has kept him in prison. And now
he's coming home a hero . . . and a stranger.*

*In the following scene Jesse and Christine are alone in
the toolshed behind her house only hours after Jesse's
return . . .*

"Jess?" Her blue eyes had grown solemn.

"What, love?"

"I don't know how to ask this . . . Jesse, I don't want to
blast things out of you that you're not ready to talk about but
I have to know . . ." An uncertain pause. "How much
haven't you told me? Was prison . . . was it horrible?"

Was it horrible? she had asked him. There she stood in
her silk knit sweater, her Gucci shoes, and one of the expensive skirts she wore that clung, but never too tightly, to her

slender thighs, asking him if prison was horrible. Her eyes were serious and bright with the fetching sincerity that seemed like such a poor defense against the darker aspects of life and that, paradoxically, always made him want to bare his soul to that uncallused sanity. The soft taut skin over her nose and cheeks shone slightly in the highly filtered light, paling her freckles, giving a fragility to her face with its combined suggestion of sturdiness and sensitivity. He would have thought four years of marriage might have banished any unease he felt about what a sociologist would label the "class difference" of their backgrounds, yet looking at her now, he had never felt it more strongly.

There was a reel of fishing line in his right hand. Where had it come from? The window shelf. He let her thick curl slide from his fingers and walked slowly to the shelf, reaching up to replace the roll, letting the motion hide his face while he spoke.

"It was a little horrible." He leaned his back against the workbench, gripping the edge. Gently shifting the focus away from himself, he said, "Was it a little horrible here without me?"

"It was a lot horrible here without you." The admission seemed to relieve some of her tension. "Not that I'm proud of being so dependent on a man, mind you."

"Say three Our Fathers, two Hail Marys, and read six months of back issues of *Ms.* magazine. Go in peace, Daughter, and sin no more." He gestured a blessing. Then, putting a palm lightly over his own heart, he added, "I had the same thing. Desolation."

"You missed the daily dose of me?"

"I missed the daily dose of you."

Her toes turned inward, freckled fingers threaded anxiously together. The round chin dropped and she gazed at him from under her lashes, a mime of bashfulness.

"So here we are—alone at last," she breathed.

Sometimes mime was a game for Christine, sometimes a refuge. In college she had joined a small troupe that passed a hat in the city parks. To combat her shyness, she still used it, retreating as though to the anonymity of whiteface and costume.

He could feel the anxiety pent up in her. *Show me you're all right, Jesse.* Something elemental in his life seemed to hinge on his comforting her. He searched desperately for the self he had been before prison, trying to clone the person she would know and recognize and feel safe with.

"Alone, and in such romantic surroundings," he said, taking a step toward her. His heel touched a shovel blade, sending a shiver of reaction through the nervously perched lawn implements that lined the wall. Some interesting quirk of physics kept them upright except for one rake that came whacking to the floor at his feet. "Ah, the hazards of these secret liaisons! We've got to stop meeting like this—the gardener is beginning to suspect."

"The gardener I can handle, but when a man in his prime is nearly cut down by a rake . . ."

"A *dangerous* rake." His voice lowered. "This, my dear, is Milwaukee's most notorious rake. More women have surrendered their virtue to him than to the legions of Caesar." He lifted the rake tines upward and made it walk toward her, giving it a lascivious whisper. "Don't fight it, *cara*. Your body was made for love. With me you can experience the fullness of your womanhood."

She laughed at his notion of the things rakes say, garnered three years ago from a teasing thumb-through of a certain deliciously fat romance novel that she had meant to keep better hidden. Raising one hand dramatically to ward off the rake, she said, "Leaf me alone, lecher!"

The rake took an offended dip and marched back to the wall in a huff. "Reject me if you must," it said in a wounded tone, "but must I endure a bad pun about my honorable profession? I thought women were supposed to love a rake," it added hopefully.

A smile hovered near the edge of her husband's mobile lips. Christine recognized a certain quality in it that made her heart beat harder. As his hands came lightly down on her shoulders, her lips parted without her will and her gaze traveled up to meet the shadow play of desire in his eyes.

"Some women prefer their very own husbands." There was a slight breathless quiver in her voice, and the throb of tightening pressure in her lungs.

"Hot damn. A compliment." Jesse let his thumbs slide down the front of her shoulders, rotating them with gentle sensuality over the soft flesh that lay above the rise of her breasts. She had begun to tremble under the sure movements of his fingers, and her slipping control brought back to him all the warm nights they had shared, the tangled sheets, the pungent musky air. He remembered the rosy flush of her upraised nipples and the way they felt on his lips. . . .

It had been so long, more than six months, since they had been together, six months since he had even seen a woman. He wondered if she realized that, or guessed how her nearness made his senses skyrocket. He wanted her to give up her body to him, to offer herself to him like an expanding breath for him to touch and taste and fill, to watch her bluebell eyes grow smoky with rapture. But though he drew her close so that he could feel the lovely fullness of her small breasts pressing into his ribs, he made no move to lower his hands or to take her lips. She seemed entrancingly clean, like a just-bathed child, and as pure. The damaged part of him came to her almost as a supplicant, unwhole before her wholesomeness. Can I touch you, love? Tell me it's all right . . .

She couldn't have heard his thoughts, or seen them, because he had learned too well to disguise them; yet her hands came to him like an answer, her fingers entwined behind his neck, pulling him toward her warm mouth. He took a breath as her lips skimmed over his and another much harder one as she stood on her toes to heighten the contact. Her tongue probed shyly at his lips and then forced an entrance, her body twisting slowly into his, a sinuous shock against his thighs.

He murmured something, random words of desire he couldn't remember as he said them; the pressure of her lips increased, and he felt thought begin to leave, and a growing pressure behind his eyelids. His hands were drifting over her blindly, as in a vision, until a shuddering fever ran through his veins and he dragged her close, pulling her hard into him, holding her there with one arm while the other slid under her sweater, his fingers spreading over the powdery softness of her skin. A surprised moan swept from her mouth into his lips as his hand lightly covered her breast. His palm absorbed her warmth, her delicate shape, and the thrillingly uneven pattern of her respiration before slipping to the fine heat and velvet distension of her nipple.

This time he heard his own whisper, telling her that he loved her, that she bewitched him, and then repeating her name again and again with the rhythm of his mouth and tongue. He was overcome, lost in her elemental femaleness, his pulse hammering through his body. Leaning her back, bringing his mouth hard against hers, he poured his kiss into her until their rapid breathing came together and he could feel every silken inch of her with the front of his body.

A keen breeze rattled the roof of the shed. It might have been the sound that brought him back, or perhaps some inner thermostat of his own, but he became aware suddenly that he was going to take her here in old man Jaroch's toolshed. And then he thought, Oh, Christ, how hard have I been holding her? His own muscles ached from the force, and he brought his head up to examine her upturned face. Sleepy lashes dusted her cheeks. A contented smile curved over damp and swollen lips. Her skin was lustrous. He pulled her into the curve of his arm with a relieved sigh, cradling her while he tried to contain his overwhelming appetite. Not here, Ludan. Not like this, with half your mind on freeze.

Kissing her once on each eyelid, he steeled his self-restraint and put her very gently from him. Her eyes flew open; her gaze leaped curiously to his.

"Heart of my heart, I'm sorry," he said softly, smiling at her, "but if I don't take my shameless hands off you . . ."

"I might end up experiencing the fullness of my womanhood in a toolshed?" she finished for him. Her returning grin had a sexy sweetness that tested his resolution. "It's not the worst idea I've ever heard."

But it is, Chris, he thought. Because enough of me hasn't walked out of that cell yet to make what would happen between us into an act of love. And the trust I see in your eyes would never allow me to give you less.

OFFICIAL RULES

To enter the sweepstakes below carefully follow all instructions found elsewhere in this offer.

The **Winners Classic** will award prizes with the following approximate maximum values: 1 Grand Prize: $26,500 (or $25,000 cash alternate); 1 First Prize: $3,000; 5 Second Prizes: $400 each; 35 Third Prizes: $100 each; 1,000 Fourth Prizes: $7.50 each. Total maximum retail value of Winners Classic Sweepstakes is $42,500. Some presentations of this sweepstakes may contain individual entry numbers corresponding to one or more of the aforementioned prize levels. To determine the Winners, individual entry numbers will first be compared with the winning numbers preselected by computer. For winning numbers not returned, prizes will be awarded in random drawings from among all eligible entries received. Prize choices may be offered at various levels. If a winner chooses an automobile prize, all license and registration fees, taxes, destination charges and, other expenses not offered herein are the responsibility of the winner. If a winner chooses a trip, travel must be complete within one year from the time the prize is awarded. Minors must be accompanied by an adult. Travel companion(s) must also sign release of liability. Trips are subject to space and departure availability. Certain black-out dates may apply.

The following applies to the sweepstakes named above:

No purchase necessary. You can also enter the sweepstakes by sending your name and address to: P.O. Box 508, Gibbstown, N.J. 08027. Mail each entry separately. Sweepstakes begins 6/1/93. Entries must be received by 12/30/94. Not responsible for lost, late, damaged, misdirected, illegible or postage due mail. Mechanically reproduced entries are not eligible. All entries become property of the sponsor and will not be returned.

Prize Selection/Validations: Selection of winners will be conducted no later than 5:00 PM on January 28, 1995, by an independent judging organization whose decisions are final. Random drawings will be held at 1211 Avenue of the Americas, New York, N.Y. 10036. Entrants need not be present to win. Odds of winning are determined by total number of entries received. Circulation of this sweepstakes is estimated not to exceed 200 million. All prizes are guaranteed to be awarded and delivered to winners. Winners will be notified by mail and may be required to complete an affidavit of eligibility and release of liability which must be returned within 14 days of date on notification or alternate winners will be selected in a random drawing. Any prize notification letter or any prize returned to a participating sponsor, Bantam Doubleday Dell Publishing Group, Inc., its participating divisions or subsidiaries, or the independent judging organization as undeliverable will be awarded to an alternate winner. Prizes are not transferable. No substitution for prizes except as offered or as may be necessary due to unavailability, in which case a prize of equal or greater value will be awarded. Prizes will be awarded approximately 90 days after the drawing. All taxes are the sole responsibility of the winners. Entry constitutes permission (except where prohibited by law) to use winners' names, hometowns, and likenesses for publicity purposes without further or other compensation. Prizes won by minors will be awarded in the name of parent or legal guardian.

Participation: Sweepstakes open to residents of the United States and Canada, except for the province of Quebec. Sweepstakes sponsored by Bantam Doubleday Dell Publishing Group, Inc., (BDD), 1540 Broadway, New York, NY 10036. Versions of this sweepstakes with different graphics and prize choices will be offered in conjunction with various solicitations or promotions by different subsidiaries and divisions of BDD. Where applicable, winners will have their choice of any prize offered at level won. Employees of BDD, its divisions, subsidiaries, advertising agencies, independent judging organization, and their immediate family members are not eligible.

Canadian residents, in order to win, must first correctly answer a time limited arithmetical skill testing question. Void in Puerto Rico, Quebec and wherever prohibited or restricted by law. Subject to all federal, state, local and provincial laws and regulations. For a list of major prize winners (available after 1/29/95): send a self-addressed, stamped envelope entirely separate from your entry to: Sweepstakes Winners, P.O. Box 517, Gibbstown, NJ 08027. Requests must be received by 12/30/94. DO NOT SEND ANY OTHER CORRESPONDENCE TO THIS P.O. BOX.

Don't miss these fabulous Bantam women's fiction titles on sale in July

CRY WOLF

☐ 56160-X $5.50/6.50 in Canada
by **Tami Hoag**
Author of STILL WATERS
A juicy novel of romantic suspense set in the steamy Louisiana Bayou by the author Publishers Weekly calls "a master of the genre."

FANTA C

☐ 56274-6 $5.99/6.99 in Canada
by **Sandra Brown**
Author of TEMPERATURES RISING
A single mother struggles to balance the needs of work, home, and the passionate desires of her own heart.

TWICE IN A LIFETIME

☐ 56298-3 $4.99/5.99 in Canada
by **Christy Cohen**
Author of PRIVATE SCANDALS
A gripping story of two women who find their friendship threatened when they each fall in love with the other's husband.

THE TESTIMONY

☐ 29948-4 $4.50/5.50 in Canada
by **Sharon and Tom Curtis**
Authors of SUNSHINE AND SHADOW
"[THE TESTIMONY] is one of the finest books I've ever read." —Romantic Times.

Ask for these books at your local bookstore or use this page to order.

☐ Please send me the books I have checked above. I am enclosing $ _____ (add $2.50 to cover postage and handling). Send check or money order, no cash or C. O. D.'s please.

Name _____

Address _____

City/ State/ Zip _____

Send order to: Bantam Books, Dept. FN109, 2451 S. Wolf Rd., Des Plaines, IL 60018
Allow four to six weeks for delivery.
Prices and availability subject to change without notice.

FN109 8/93